MW00936900

SAVAGE BROTHERS MC BOOK 3

Jordan Marie

Editor
Twin Sisters Rocking Book Reviews
Fran Owen & CJ Fling

Copyright © 2015
Print Edition

All rights reserved. No part of this publication may be reproduced, distributed, or transmitted in any form or by any means, including photocopying, recording, or other electronic or mechanical methods, without the prior written permission of the author.

WARNING: The unauthorized reproduction or distribution of this copyrighted work is illegal. No part of this book may be scanned, uploaded or distributed via the internet or any other means, electronic or print, without the publisher's/author's permission. Criminal copyright infringement, including infringement without monetary gain, is investigated by the FBI and is punishable by up to 5 years in federal prison and a fine of 250,000.00 (http://www.fbi.gov/ipr/). Please purchase only authorized electronic or print editions and do not participate or encourage the electronic piracy of copyrighted material. Your respect of the author's rights is appreciated.

This book is a work of fiction and any resemblance to persons, living or dead, or places events or locales is purely coincidental. The characters are created from the author's imagination and used in a fictitious manner.

Cover:
Designer: Margreet Asselbergs – Rebel Edit Designs .
Photos Used for cover purchased through Dollar Photo Club
Additional Editing Services Provided by KA Matthews / K J Book Promotions

Trademarks:

Any brands, titles, artists, lyrics, quotes, etc. used in this book were mentioned purely for artistic purposes and are either used as a product of the author's imagination or used fictitiously. None of the herein mentioned products, authors artists etc., endorse this book whatsoever and the author acknowledges their trademarked status which has been used in this work of fiction.

Author acknowledges trademarked status or owners of various products and further acknowledges that said use is not authorized or endorsed by said owners. While some places in this book might mention actual areas or places, author acknowledges that it was purely for entertainment purposes and not endorsed by owners or has nothing to do with actual place and was mentioned to further reader's enjoyment only.

This e-book is licensed for your personal enjoyment only. It is not to be re-sold or given away to others and doing so is a violation of the copyright.

Warning
The Content in this book is graphic and intended for mature audiences only. 18+ and above only. Contains sexual violence, sexual situations, violence, excessive profanity and death. Reader should please read with that knowledge.

Author's Note:
This book is part of an ongoing series. While it can be read as a standalone it is highly recommended that you have read Volume 1 of the Savage Brothers MC series, *Breaking Dragon*. Volume 2, *Saving Dancer*, while not as closely linked to the main characters will also provide more character detail that is useful when reading.

Dedication

This book is dedicated to all who have had a part, both large and small, in helping me live my dream. From a note of encouragement to the purchase of the book and anything in between, there are no words I can offer except a heartfelt thank you.

For the readers who have opened their hearts and minds to embrace Dragon and Nicole, please note this book was meant to be a celebration of their love. A short novella to celebrate their wedding. Dragon, as he often does, had other plans. The direction it went into was not planned, and for the life of me I cannot write with an outline. It's a wild, crazy and emotional journey which took it way out of the realm of a wedding book. It takes a village to write a book seems appropriate for me. Please read to the end to see my list of acknowledgments; for the wonderful people in my corner.

I hope you enjoy the story, I'm not ashamed to say it's my favorite of all I have written both in this series and in the past.

Jordan.

Table of Contents

LOVING NICOLE

Savage Brothers MC Series

Book 3

Jordan Marie

Prologue

MICHAEL

New York
Three Weeks Earlier

I PUSH MY chair back, tilting it while bringing my feet up. I rest them on my desk. My eyes follow the perfect crease in my three thousand dollar Armani suit. You have to pay for perfection, demand it. From where I am sitting I can see my secretary buttoning up her black, silk blouse.

A shame really, because it will ultimately cover up the marks I left on her body only moments earlier. I came oh so close to choking the life out of her. She blacked out this time. Just the memory of it causes my dick to jump and I wonder how quickly I can finish this call. Will I have time to take her again, before my next meeting? Maybe I'll force her to suck me off and hide under my desk. If she's a good little dog, I'll give her what she wants later. She's always begging for it. As dangerous as I am, she still craves more. It's good, it's an aphrodisiac knowing she's getting off on it—but only because it makes me push it farther. I have to, because if not, I don't get to see the fear in her eyes and motherfucker, I crave the fear.

"Hurry Donald, I have someone waiting on me."

At my words my secretary turns and looks at me, her brown eyes flash in understanding.

I take my feet down, slide my seat back another couple of inches and motion under my desk. She walks towards me, but I shake my head no. She stops instantly, such a good little pet.

Naked. I mouth the word. She nods her understanding and begins undressing.

"Mr. Kavanagh, we've found her."

I freeze. The little bitch has been missing for five fucking years.

"Where?" I demand, waving my secretary off. My dick being jammed down her throat is the last thing on my mind now. She picks up her clothes and quickly exits, having seen this mood enough to know to run for cover.

"She's in a small town in Eastern Kentucky."

"No fucking way."

"Yes sir, do we apprehend her and bring her to you?"

I consider this, as it would be the easiest and ultimately the cleanest alternative. But alas, I do not do clean nor easy.

"No. Watch her, evaluate the situation. I want pictures tonight. I will decide after that."

"Yes sir, there might be one slight issue."

My hand tightens on the receiver. I will not have anything stand in my way now. It will not happen.

"That is?" I prompt.

"She seems to have taken up with a gang."

"A gang? That does not sound like Melinda. Perhaps your incompetence is showing again, Donald."

"No sir, the hair is different, but this is definitely Mrs. Kavanagh."

"A gang?"

"A motorcycle gang. I believe they call themselves the Savage Brothers."

A motorcycle gang? Well, well, my Melinda never ceases to amaze, too bad I'm going to kill her.

"I expect a detailed report tonight. Do not disappoint, Donald."

"Yes, sir."

I hang the phone up and turn my seat around to stare at the skyline of downtown Manhattan. The different shapes and sizes of the skyscrapers jut and point in a peculiar pattern, which is strangely beautiful. The water in the distance is calm and the blue reflects the sun's glare. My hands tighten on the arms of my leather cushioned chair.

Finally, Melinda is in my grasp. I vow she will not get away this time.

Chapter 1

DRAGON

I COME AWAKE slowly, my eyes adjusting to the dim light in the room. A smile hits my face as I feel my woman's lips graze my stomach.

"Morning, Mama."

"Mmmm…," she moans against my skin, her tongue darting in and out of my belly button.

I run my fingers through her hair, caressingly. I love her hair; the color, the texture, the way it always feels so soft between my fingers. I feel her teeth rake across my skin. She places a teasing bite on my stomach at the same exact time her hand cups my balls, gently massaging them.

I wrap her hair tighter around my fingers. Fuck, yeah. My girl has been horny as hell this last month. She says it's because of the pregnancy. All I know is I get to fuck her, sometimes, five times a day and I love every damn second of it; even when I can do nothing but get her off with my fingers, because my dick is exhausted. I'm one happy motherfucker. Hell, I might keep her knocked up constantly if this is the reward.

"My Mama needing me to make her come?" I ask. Her head slowly raises, she looks up with those gorgeous blue eyes of hers, and they lock on mine.

"No," she says with a smile, her voice warm, husky and full of need. Her hand goes to my cock, pumping it with a firm grip. Her thumb grazing the slick head with each downward stroke.

"No?" I ask confused, because her actions are not going along with the denial.

"No, I want you to come," she corrects me and bam, just like that, I feel my release so close a cold sweat breaks out on me.

This woman has so much power over me and it's been like that since the first time I kissed her and felt her ass in my hands. She branded me and destroyed me for any other woman.

"Climb on board, Mama." We've switched to having her on top most of the time when we make love because I'm afraid of hurting the baby. She's six months along now, and fuck, she's gorgeous—more beautiful every damned day. The sight of her stomach swelled and tight with our baby, her large breasts even bigger—preparing for our child all of the subtle changes in her that I can't begin to list…all those put together and Nicole, herself, captivates me. Every day I find something new to love that I want to explore with her.

Nicole ignores my demand and instead, slides farther down between my legs and before I can gather my brain cells to say one more thing, her mouth is sliding down my staff and she's sucking on my cock with a growl. My head pushes back against my pillow and my eyes close. I take a minute to just relish the feeling of being owned by this amazing woman and the hot, wet, slick depths of her mouth.

Nothing better. There is nothing better than being with Nicole. That is the one sane thought I can muster as she picks up her pace and starts sucking my cock harder, in tandem with her hand stroking me and controlling the depth.

She's been waking me up every day like this. I haven't told her that there are times I wake up before her and pretend I am still sleeping, just waiting for her mouth. I close my eyes, enjoying the feel of her tongue sliding along my dick. Reveling in the soft, wet, slow slide as her tongue flattens and licks me so fucking good I can barely hold on. When it flicks over the head, darting hungrily to gather all the pre-cum that is dripping from me, I can take no more.

My hands go under her arms and I lift, pulling her up so fast that she is quickly straddling me. Nicole works with me and uses her hand to guide me inside. I groan as I slip into silky depths. I do my best to remember to hold her back. My woman is fucking greedy, if I don't watch her, she will slam down on me until I bottom out inside of her. It'd feel fucking fantastic, but I don't want to do anything that may harm the baby. The changes in the way I give her my cock are driving her crazy. I know that's part of the reason she's been waking me up every morning with my own personal form of *happy ending*.

I can't help it though. The thought of a part of the two of us growing inside of Nicole is a miracle to me. A beautiful miracle that I never thought I would experience. The fact that I'm sharing it with a woman who owns a piece of my soul? A woman who I'm so fucking wrapped up in, I will never get free? Shit, that's so far into the miracle zone I can't even fucking believe it.

"Dragon..." Nicole whimpers and I know it's because I've used my hands on her hips to slowly lower her on me. See? Greedy.

"Damn Mama, do you feel how your pussy is already trying to milk me dry? You want my cum, don't you?" I growl as I feel her inner muscles clench on my dick, compressing and releasing so slow and tightly that it is divine torture. I never want it to end.

Nicole begins her ride in earnest now. Sliding up and down on me, the room echoing with the combined sounds of our breathing, moans and the slick suction of our union. Up and down and on each downward stroke she curls and rotates, while bearing down on my cock so firmly, I know I make some kind of unintelligible noise, I just couldn't tell you what it is.

My hands are cupping her swollen breasts. The nipples have darkened and grown. They fascinate me these days. They're so ultra-sensitive that I've been able to make her come doing nothing but torturing them for an hour or so. It's a fun game that I make note to play again later today. It's my contribution to making sure the baby is strong. It always wears her out enough, she takes a mid-day nap.

I lean up to run my tongue along one of her nipples; it has hardened so much it looks physically painful. I use my thumb to graze against the other one. Her hands wrap around my head pulling me closer with such force, my dick is as rigid as stone when I thrust up into her. Fuck, it turns me on knowing she needs me this much. She is *mine*.

I switch nipples and use my thumb and forefinger to torture the moistened one I leave behind. Nicole's ride somehow picks up speed, the movements she makes are jerky and not as controlled. Her breathing is erratic, her head is thrown back, her soft blonde hair glistens in the pale sunlight, and the ends tease my legs.

Fucking phenomenal and mine, *all mine*. I'll kill a motherfucker if he even tries to touch her.

That thought fragments into a thousand pieces as she comes. I feel her wet, slick cream sliding over me. She's using my cock so hungrily, I'm immediately pulled along with her and unload so hard inside of her—I think I might die on the spot.

Heaven. This is the closest I'll ever get to the place. When I am with Nicole, when I am inside of her, when I am fucking her, when she is begging for my cum? *That* is my heaven.

Nicole collapses against me, angling so that her head can rest against my neck and shoulder. Her lips touch my jawline and chin before she settles against me.

"I'm pretty sure Heaven has angels singing, pearly gates, and golden streets…not your woman's pussy, sweetheart." She yawns against my skin.

Shit, I didn't realize I spoke the words out loud. I kiss the top of her head. My hand rubbing the side of her stomach where our child is resting.

Every. Damn. Day.

Every day since Nicole has come into my life just gets better, happier, and fuller. I don't even know how that shit is possible, but I am completely happy. Hell, I even yawn along with her. It's no shame. My woman wears me out—in all good ways.

"That's the reason it's also the only heaven I want,

Mama. An eternity without my woman's pussy? Fuck that. You and I will make our own afterlife."

She laughs I think. I can't be sure because her lips are buried against the pulse in my neck and she yawns at the same time.

"You didn't let me finish sucking you off again. I want your cum, Dragon."

"I gave it to you, woman."

"You know what I'm saying Dragon, don't play dumb," she says while her hand wraps loose around my stomach, she slides off my cock and wraps one leg over my hip.

"Told you Nicole, my boy ain't about to taste my cum."

"And I told you, that's not how it works…"

"I heard you, but I think about it when you're sucking me and I can't let go. So, this is how I'm gonna play it."

"I'm going to keep trying. One day you'll be so far gone, you will give me your cum before you think about it. I just need to get more inventive."

"Woman, I think you've tapped the market on inventive, unless you're thinking about bringing another party into our bed."

"I'd gut a bitch who tried to get near your cock. Hell, any part of you. Fuck, even our bed. I'd gut her and dance on her entrails."

I laugh as I hear my words, words I've used come back at me.

"Woman, you're starting to sound like me."

"It's a problem, but I deal with it. Back to the issue at hand though, another woman is not getting near you, hmmm, another man though…"

"I'd cut off his cock and feed it to him, then gut him and feed a piece of him to the vultures every fucking day for a year."

"So, I think it's safe to say we're not going to be having a threesome anytime soon."

"Ever. Not fucking ever."

She laughs and I can't help the smile that comes over my face.

"You know we might want to keep the whole entrails and gutting talk to a minimum, so Junior doesn't hear. I'm pretty sure that's more likely to happen than him ingesting daddy's baby gravy."

I bark out in laughter at that. Shit this woman kills me. I never laughed before her. Never.

"You are one wacky bitch, Mama."

"My man, always so sweet and free-flowing with the compliments. Shut up Dragon, and let me go to sleep."

"Go to sleep, Mama. I love you."

"Forever," she whispers against my neck.

"Forever Nicole, forever."

In just mere minutes her breathing evens out and she sleeps. I just lie here, holding her close and enjoying this moment—like I always do. This is my time. My time for giving thanks to the man above for giving me Nicole and not taking her away. Time for me to just hold the one person in this entire world who will ever own me, except maybe our son and any future children.

Nicole and I are having a baby. A beautifully healthy baby boy. I close my eyes, my hand still moving along the side of her stomach. We've had two of those ultrasound things now and you can see the baby clearly. 3D or 4D, I'm not sure what they call it, all I know is it gave me a picture of our beautiful, innocent child.

I have the world. I have the world here in my hands. My woman and my baby—it doesn't get any better than this. It's all I never really knew I wanted, until now.

"Forever, Mama," I whisper, as I slowly let sleep claim me. It's not quite daylight and after a workout like that, I need to hold my woman and rest. I feel my son kick against my hand and fall asleep with a smile on my face.

Chapter 2

NICOLE

I'M USED TO waking up alone by now, but I always miss him. Dragon. I watched this movie once, a long time ago, about soulmates. It was a cheesy, corny movie but it talked about souls being separated when they are brought into this world and how they spend their entire existence here on Earth, trying to find their missing partner. I always loved the idea. I never dreamed it was real, but with Dragon that scenario doesn't seem far-fetched. I find myself praying that my child finds his woman, the one woman who will complete him as Dragon does me—and good lord, if that isn't a syrupy, sugary load of crap to be thinking about first thing in the morning. Dani's right, pretty soon rainbows will be shooting out of my ass.

I pat my stomach gently and slowly get up. I'm hungry. That's nothing new, I swear Junior has me eating everything that's not nailed down. This morning he's demanding bacon before I even get fully awake.

"Nic! You up?" I hear the panic in Dani's voice, even through the door.

"Come on in," I call out, because it's going to take me awhile to even get up off the bed. Junior is already making that difficult. I'm wondering how I'm going to manage the last few months, at this rate.

"Nic!" Dani walks in, her dark hair pulled high on her head in a ponytail, her face made up perfectly with her trademark dark red lipstick. She's dressed in jeans that look worn out, but if truth was known she bought them just yesterday. She may have left her past behind, but my girl has a designer taste. She is wearing a purple, white and black checkered flannel shirt. You would think that shirt wouldn't go with the vibe she has going on, but somehow it totally does. Dani's always been like that, I've always been a little envious.

"Dani, please don't give me shit about the dresses again. I gave in and let you have…"

"Nic, please."

The desperation in Dani's voice causes my heart to trip. This is way more serious than the length of a damn maid of honor dress.

"What…"

It's the only word I can get out. I'm too busy taking in the stark fear shining in her brown eyes. Panic grabs me, because there's only one thing that could cause this much fear on Dani's face.

"Mich…"

She pushes a rumpled, wadded, white paper at me, and stops me from finishing. That's okay, I'd rather not say that monster's name ever again. I have a bad feeling, which only gets stronger when I notice how hard Dani's hands are shaking. I lick my suddenly dry lips. This is not good. Slowly my attention moves from Dani down to the letter in my hand, the one I've slowly been unfolding without even realizing it. I stretch out the hopeless wrinkles, move my hands against them and press hard into my leg. I'm putting off opening it. I'm not ashamed to say I'm afraid; if the look on Dani's face is anything to go by, I have reason to be.

Again, I lick my lips, damn my mouth is dry. I pick the paper up, not surprised to see my hands are shaking too. It's torn out of a magazine. I look at it confused. I'm not sure what I was expecting, but this isn't it. It's a copy of a society paper from New York years ago. On the cover is a picture of Dani, a much younger and definitely more innocent Dani, but Dani nonetheless. The paper is yellow from time, but the headline under it jumps out at you—or at least it does me. It causes my heart to lodge in my throat.

Society darling, Melinda Marinetti to marry Michael Kavanagh

Oh fuck. Oh fuck, no.

"Where did you get this?" I ask and I hate that I can't keep the panic out of my voice. Dani doesn't need to hear my panic.

"My car."

"Maybe you left it…"

"It was on the windshield. How the fuck did he find me? I have to leave! I can't stay here anymore!"

I crumple the paper in my hands. The happy, sweet face of the young girl with innocent brown eyes and broad smile mocks me. I miss that girl. She was swallowed by a darkness and pain so deep, that I'll never find her. It took me a year, but I finally acknowledged it—that girl was lost to me forever.

"You do not have to leave! Right here is the safest place for you, Dani! Dragon and the boys would protect you with their lives!"

Dani flops down on the bed beside me and I hate the tears that are falling down her face. Michael took way too much from her already, and he shouldn't get any more of her tears.

"Don't you think I know that? Hell, half the men here still haven't forgiven me for putting you in danger, but they would protect me. I can't ask them to do that, Nic."

"You won't have to ask Dani, we're family…"

"Nic, Michael won't rest until he has killed every member of the Savage Brothers and he'll make sure it is painful," Dani responds, and I know she's right.

"Dragon can handle him…we have to tell him."

"I can't. I won't. I've caused enough shit. Fuck, I almost got you killed. You have to promise me you won't tell him, Nic."

"Dani, you have to let the past go." A day hasn't gone by that she hasn't apologize for the mess with Tiny.

"It might be alright for you but it's not for me, and it sure as hell is not okay with Dragon. What I did was stupid and we almost lost our lives because of it. All because Dragon reminded me of Michael!"

"Dragon is nothing like Michael," I feel the need to defend, because I don't like that she ever thought of Dragon like that.

"Don't you think I know that now? Hell Nic, I knew it then on some level, but my brain and mind…they don't work right when it comes to Michael. Nothing works right…"

"I can tell Dragon, he'll understand…"

"No!" She screams out in panic. "Promise me you won't tell him! Promise me Nic, or I'll leave right now. I don't want anyone to know! Please!!!"

"Dani, you have to forgive yourself. I'm alive, you're alive and we're okay."

"We are now, but Michael knows where I'm at, no one will be safe. He doesn't know you're involved, Nic. If he finds out, he'll take it personal. You covered for me, you *lied* to him. Michael won't accept that. I have to leave, it's the only solution. If I leave he'll follow me and leave you alone."

"Dani, I'm getting married in two weeks!"

"I know. I'll try and stay Nic, but I can't put anyone in danger and…oh god, Nic, I can't let Michael find me again. I can't…"

Her tears fall harder and the sobs shake her body. I wrap her up in my arms and hug her closely, letting her cry. It takes all I have not to join her.

"We'll figure this out. I promise we will." I'm saying it, but even I'm not sure I mean it. I need to tell Dragon, but I won't betray Dani. She's had enough of that in her life. If I betray her, she'll completely withdraw. I'll lose her forever.

I feel like I'm between a rock and a hard place here. I really don't know what to do. So, for now, I hold Dani close and let her shed more tears over a monster who doesn't deserve them. The only thing he deserves is death.

Chapter 3

DRAGON

I'M GOING TO be a fucking married man in two weeks. How is that shit possible? How did I get here? When I look back on the wild ride that Nicole and I have shared, I can barely believe it. I look over at her and Dani. They're huddled up in the corner, thick as thieves. Normally, this would make me worry—especially with Dani involved, but I figure it is okay for now. Probably more damn wedding talk. I never knew women could go off the deep end over this shit. Damn woman had me sitting for two fucking hours picking out a cake, which seems ridiculous since she ended up picking chocolate. I mean hell, why did I try a thousand other flavors I had no idea existed, just to end up on chocolate?

"That looks like trouble," Crush says sitting down beside me and angling his chair so he can watch Nicole and Dani's huddle.

"Probably making sure they have the right damn shade of pink for napkins," I say, only half joking.

"Fuck me, pink? Prez man, it's bad enough you're asking us to put on monkey suits, I'll be damned if I will sit at a table surrounded by pink frilly shit."

"I was thinking of making sure your new cut was pink," I respond, taking a swig of beer.

Crusher throws up his middle finger after choking on his beer and I can't help but grin. I smile a lot more these days.

"Heard from Dance?" Crush asks, his eyes still glued to the women.

"Yeah, he and Red will be back in town this weekend. They're staying with Mary for a few more days."

"He seems better."

"Yeah, having Red in his corner seems to have helped."

"It's tearing Bull up, brother."

"He'll be alright."

"Maybe, but he's pretty messed up over Carrie."

"Jesus, Crush. When did you become such a meddling busybody?"

"Fuck you, just making observations."

"Yeah, well, I'm making some of my own."

Crush turns and looks at me and it's the first time since he sat down here, that I have his attention.

"What's that?" He asks taking another drink of his beer. He tries to appear at ease, but his body is tight and I can tell he's tense as hell.

"Don't go there Crush, that woman is nothing but trouble, bro." It's honest advice, I don't figure he'll take it, but I'm going to give it. You'd have to be a fucking moron not to notice the way he's panting after Nic's girl.

"Have no idea what you are talking about, Drag."

"Like hell. You want to stick your dick in Dani, but fuck man. A woman like that? You get your dick in her, it might feel good for a minute or two, but definitely not worth the shit-storm that will follow."

"I'm thinking I could make it feel a lot better than just good and definitely longer than a minute or two."

"Whatever man. With a woman like that you're liable to draw back a stub. That woman has issues."

"What woman doesn't?" He asks and I can't help but follow Crush's lead and look over at the women still huddled in deep discussion.

"Nic, she gives me calm not drama. That's the kind of woman you need, brother."

"They don't look calm right now," Crush says.

"As long as Nicole's drama is over what fucking shade of white the cake frosting should be? I'm cool," I respond.

"There are shades of white?"

"Who the fuck knew, right? I swear this whole wedding thing may be the death of me."

I sit there in silence for a little while, my eyes still watching my woman. I glance at Crush and notice he is doing much the same with Dani. This doesn't exactly fill me with warm, fuzzy feelings. Nic hasn't shared a lot about Dani, other than to stress how important she is to her. I was pissed as hell after the bitch put Nic in danger—hell she put herself in danger as well. Still, Nic told me Dani had a life I didn't know anything about, that had left some deep scars. I know all about trying to survive a past that scarred you. Fuck, every member of the Savage Brothers does. So, I promised as long as the bitch didn't cause more problems, I'd be cool. I mean it, but if Crush starts something up with her and she fucks with my brother's head…

I trail off in my thoughts as I notice Torch coming in from the back office. Torch is a new face around here. Striker and Gunner decided to re-up with Uncle Sam. It wasn't a big surprise, both men have wanderlust in them. I personally think they'd make better nomads than patched in members. The lure of the open road always called to them more than the rest of us. So we slowly moved Hawk up the ranks more and patched in Frog. Nailer and Six are still prospects, though we are going to have to remedy that soon. Both men have proven their loyalty to the club in spades, especially during everything with Dancer. Still, the mess with Dancer and how an enemy managed to catch us with our pants down, pisses me the hell off. I don't care if the man did have the power to disappear for months on end, without a trace. It doesn't matter if he had a degree in electronics and connections in the underground. I will not fucking let my men be caught unaware again. So, I did something I thought I would never do. I talked to Skull about it.

Skull and I have shit in common, even if I don't want to admit it. Plus, being a President of a MC is not a fucking walk in the park. You carry a heavy weight on your shoulders. You make decisions that mean life and death to men and women you care about—your family. So, despite the motherfucker's preoccupation with my woman, he and I have struck up a strange kind of truce.

Torch isn't a member of the Savage crew. He actually is a patched in member of Skull's crew. He is a fucking genius at making state of the art security systems. It helped that he and Freak seemed to just immediately gel. So I asked him to come in and help beef up our defenses. I can handle a lot of shit. I have no problem when it comes to guns, ammo and man power. Yet, this new age shit and the computers and high tech gadgetry are beyond me. Savage MC is a club that needs all its bases covered. I will not allow one more fucking person to take me or my men by the balls.

It's essential I make a statement. I need to make sure I have men around me that understand that and are willing to make some big ass moves towards becoming the major power, not only in my town, but in the state. So, with the alliance between Savage MC and Devil's Fire solid, Torch, Gavel and some hulk called Beast have all become regular fixtures at my damn club. Sadly, even Skull is here more often than not—which is okay as long as he doesn't speak to my woman.

"Yo! Dragon. We got problems, man. Freak and I need to see you in the back."

My easy going mood vanishes immediately. Damn it, we've barely recovered from the drama with Dance and motherfucking *Francis*. I need quiet. I do *not* need more fucking drama. I get up and walk towards Torch, making note that Crusher falls in step behind me with a muttered curse.

I find myself hoping my day isn't about to be shot all to hell.

Chapter 4

NICOLE

FEAR GRABS ME when I hear Torch's words. Has Michael done something else? I see the color bleed out of Dani's face and I know she fears the same thing. I grab hold of her hand and try to reassure her. Dani comes off all badass and attitude, but she's very delicate since Michael. He changed her. If I have enjoyed anything about the heartbreaking journey she's taken over the last few years, it has been watching her stretch her wings again. I might not agree with the things she does and the choices she makes, but I know she makes them because she needs to prove she doesn't answer to anyone. In some small way it helps her gain independence. You had to see how broken and empty she was at one point to clearly understand.

"You bitches about ready to head out?" Lips asks, as her and Nikki walk over. We are so deep in thought over Michael, neither of us noticed them. Both of us jump in reaction. Luckily neither woman seems to notice it—or at least they don't bring it up.

"Go?" I ask and I know my voice is squeaky and strained.

"Yeah bitch, it's our last fitting? Those damn pink dresses you're making us squeeze our asses into?" Nikki complains.

Oh shit, I completely forgot about it.

"Yeah, give me a minute to tell Dragon bye and we'll head out." I try to smile reassuringly at Dani and walk down the hall to Dragon's office.

I don't knock on the door immediately, I stand outside and try to listen. Is that not messed up? Trying to listen to what my man is saying? I hate the feeling it gives me. I hate Michael all over again. I thought we were done with him. What kind of mad man doesn't give up after years… hell, almost five fucking years? Oh yeah, a lunatic, that's who!

I can't hear a damn thing through the heavy door. My hand goes to the doorknob. What would happen if I open it slightly, just to hear? Would Dragon notice? I start to do it, when the door opens and Dragon is standing in front of me. My heart beats in triple time. Does he know what I'm thinking? Does he know what is happening?

"Nicole? What's going on, Mama?"

Fear, intense and real, and I haven't even done anything yet! Still, that's the feeling that swamps me. I try to swallow it down.

"I…I wanted to say goodbye to you. We're headed out to the fitting." Does he notice how I'm not looking him in the eye? I can't do this. I'm going to talk to Dani. I can't keep things from Dragon. Besides, Michael is dangerous. Dragon needs to know, to be prepared.

His finger reaches under my chin and pulls my face up so that our eyes meet.

"You okay, Mama? Camera showed you were out here for a while. You're not sick are you? Do you need me?"

"I…I'm good," I say swallowing down the guilt as I take in the concern on his face. "I love you, Dragon."

He smiles, and like always, his smile and the way it makes those deep brown eyes of his light up, warms me. God, this man is beautiful.

"What do you say I make you late for your fitting?" He asks, his fingers gently stroking the side of my face.

"How late?" I whisper, not really caring.

He grabs the cheeks of my ass and pulls me up on his body. Because of my pregnancy it takes some work but I semi-wrap my legs around him and lock my arms around his neck. I bury my face into the side of his neck and just breathe him in. Dragon is home. The only home I've ever known or wanted.

"We'll send your girls on and they can do it without you."

It's so tempting and I really want to, but I feel guilty. I should stick close to Dani. Dragon's kissing along the side of my neck. He bites the lobe of my ear and flicks his tongue over it and I lose focus. We walk back through the front room of the club. The club members instantly start their hollering and ribbing. You would think they would get accustomed to Dragon and me by now. I can't even count how many times he's run people out of the room so he could bend me over the bar. Apparently, today, he'd rather take me back to our room. I'm totally okay with that.

"Woman! We're going to be late!" I hear Lips yell in the background.

"I need you riding my cock, Mama. I can't wait to feel that greedy pussy of yours sinking down on me." Dragon whispers in my ear to distract me. I love that my man has such a filthy mouth. Sometimes, I think I can come from his words alone.

"Give me ten minutes!" I holler back in the direction of my girls. Wishing my stomach was just a little smaller because I can't bend down and torture his nipples like I want. I miss the days when I was more flexible, especially when it comes to our lovemaking.

Dragon's hands bite into the cheeks of my ass.

"Fuck, Mama, I'm going to need more than ten minutes."

"Make that thirty minutes," I call back and somehow I can hear Dragon's soft laugh over the hard beating of my heart and the yelling by the club members.

"Mama, thirty minutes will barely get us started."

I smile against his throat and then lean to whisper in his ear.

"I think you can do it if you try really hard."

"I get much harder and you won't be able to walk when we're done."

"Promises, promises."

"Nicole, you're always busting my ass," he says laughing as we cross the threshold to our room and he uses his body and foot to close the door to our room.

He lays me on the bed and, for just this one minute, I forget all about Dani and the problems coming our way and just enjoy being with my man—my soon-to-be-husband.

"Have I told you today how much I love you, Dragon?"

He stands over me, his eyes on mine and I know in that moment there has never been a time when I have loved him more.

"Are you okay, Mama?" He asks.

"When I'm with you, I'm perfect," I answer truthfully.

"This pregnancy is making my woman emotional," he says using his thumb to wipe away a tear that falls from my eye.

I can't help the tears. I should be telling Dragon every-thing that's going on, and I *really* shouldn't be hiding things from him. I really shouldn't be spying on him. If he knew, it would hurt him; destroy him. Just the thought brings another tear. I'll tell Dani this evening. I have to let Dragon know, I can't keep secrets from him.

"Make love to me, Dragon," I beg needing his touch to wipe the rest of the world away—at least for now.

Chapter 5

DRAGON

I WATCH AS my woman piles into the SUV that Crusher is driving. She's riding in the back with Dani and Nikki. Lips is riding up front. Something is off and I'm not sure what it is. It's weighing my woman down heavily and I don't like it. I couldn't get her to talk to me about it, but I haven't given up; I'll get it out of her eventually. It's probably just wedding stuff. Lord knows it's stressing me out, and I don't even give a fuck about it. Hell, long as my ring ends up on Nicole's finger, I'm good.

"Yo! Boss, we got that information you asked for," Torch calls, claiming my attention. With one last glance at my woman, I turn around.

I have this damn feeling in the pit of my stomach. I can't explain what it is, but it feels like I'm a bundle of nerves and my skin is crawling, like I'm being watched. It's instinct. A skill honed in blood and death when I served overseas. It's never let me down, so I know there is shit about to hit the fan. It fucking pisses me off. Ever since Irish's betrayal it's been one thing after another—like the motherfucker put a damned curse on the club. It's made worse, because I miss the fucking traitor. Every-fucking-day, I miss him. What kind of screwed up shit is that? I've never admitted that to anyone, not even Nicole. What man leads others and misses a traitor, like he was still a brother? It wars in my brain. There are days I want to shed tears for the fucker. His screams haunt me, and then there are other days I want him back here, so I can fucking kill him again.

I look around at the sour faces in my office and hell, I know my day is only going to get worse. Earlier, the boys had found footage of a stranger prowling around the outside of the fence surrounding the club. The man seemed to be taking pictures. He stayed in the shadows and used a zoom lens, so he never got close enough for us to get a good picture of him. I was hoping when Torch told me he had information for me, we had somehow managed to find out who the fucker was. From the look on the faces around me, I'm thinking that's not happening.

"Spill it."

Frog, Freak, Torch, and Hawk are sitting around the table and not a damned one of them looks happy. Again, I feel sadness. None of my brothers I bled and fought with are here. Bull is back from the rehab, but he's not the same. Hell, he's not even here at the meeting. No one has seen him today. He leaves early and doesn't get back until late in the night. When he is here, he talks to no one. I'm going to have to deal with it soon. I can't allow it to get to the point it did with Dance…

"Well, one of you motherfuckers start talking. I got shit to do," I growl, more because I can't seem to shut my brain down these days.

"Yeah, like finding a monkey suit," Freak returns.

"Screw you, I didn't hear you telling Nikki no."

"Woman sucked my dick like a Hoover, didn't have the brains left to say no," Freak jokes.

I slap him on the back of the head, not arguing, because that's pretty much how Nicole gets her way.

"So, what the fuck is going on?"

"Someone was prowling around the Den last night. First we thought it was just a drunk wandering around in the parking lot, but not many drunks in this area that we don't know."

"True."

"Sure aren't any drunks around here who wear expensive suits," Freak adds, punching some buttons on his keyboard and the screen zooms in on an older man, maybe in his late forties, with a suit and hat on. His steps are sure, not drunk at all and everything about him screams that he is on alert. He keeps glancing over his back to see if he is being followed. His head is tucked close and aimed at an angle that's next to impossible to get a good view of his face. *Shit.*

"Can you get a look at his face at all?" I ask watching as he walks toward Nicole's old Mercedes that Dani drives now.

I made Nicole switch to one of the club's Tahoes. The safety rating is better and it has more room for the baby; plus, it's four wheel drive. She bitched and moaned, but gave in eventually.

"There's a sketchy picture of his face, as he walks back to the club. This camera is on the outside light overlooking employee parking," Freak answers.

"What's he doing?"

"He's putting a note on the windshield of Dani's car,

you can't really see it," Freak says.

"Maybe he's just trying to pick her up? Lot of those men get attached to the dancers," Frog joins in.

"Possible, though Dani's not mentioned anything happening that was unusual."

"Bitch wouldn't," Torch says, and Freak throws an elbow into him.

I don't understand it, but Dani and Freak seem to have formed this weird platonic friendship. Or at least I think it is. Hell, as jealous as Nikki is, if it isn't, we'll find Dani dead in a ditch somewhere. That bitch is *not* one to mess with.

"I would have gone with the stalker fan theory, but watch what the son of a bitch does here."

As soon as Freak gets the sentence out, we watch as the man squats down and monkeys under the car.

"Lo-jack?"

Freak motions to Hawk and Hawk hands me a small black box. A tracker, and a pretty expensive one. We've used them from time to time in the club. So much for hoping the club had dealt with enough drama for a while. *Fuck.*

"It could still be a crazy stalker," Hawk says.

"To afford that kind of technology?" Freak questions and he knows exactly how expensive the little toy I'm holding costs. Our club has spent a crap-load on them in the past.

"So, he's a crazy-rich-off-his-ass Stalker," Hawk responds, but you can tell he's not convinced. I'm not either.

I keep watching the screen, holding the tracker in my hand. The guy makes it through the parking lot almost to the front of the Den and raises his head briefly. Freak freezes the image on the screen. It's piss-poor quality but you can see him even through the shaded, grainy picture. Trouble is, I don't recognize him at all.

"Is he the same guy that was sneaking around the outside gates before?"

"The build is def' the same. I'd say it is Drag, but there's no way to be sure," Torch responds.

"Beef up security. Have the prospects watching like their lives depend on it. Fuck, if we have some more shit hitting the club, their lives *will* depend on it." I growl and stomp out of the room.

I'm pissed. I think Nicole knows what's going on. I just don't understand why she hasn't talked to me about it. I'm going to have to have some words with her about it all. It pisses me off even more that once again it is her girl causing drama. I hope I'm wrong. I really fucking hope that I am, and Dani is not about to cause another fucking shit-storm to hit the club.

That dread I've been feeling clawing at my gut? The one where it feels like there are shoes hanging over my head about to drop? That feeling tells me I'm not wrong.

Chapter 6

NICOLE

THE THING ABOUT dreams? They never seem to work out like you want them to. I'm in the middle of Mountain Bridal, with my best girls around me (save Carrie, who will be back this weekend) and I'm miserable. I'm *miserable* because Dani has retreated back into the woman who begged me for help all those years ago. I'm *miserable* because I tried to spy on my future-husband. I'm *miserable* because in a round-about way I lied to him. Most of all, I'm completely *miserable,* because there is this wall between Dragon and I now. A wall *I* put there. A wall *I* need to break down and smash into a hundred thousand different pieces.

I can't, not until I can draw Dani out of this place she's withdrawn to. I can't even touch it right now though, there are too many around us. Trying will only bring disaster, because Nikki and Lips will hear. If I tell anyone what is going on, it will be Dragon. I just wish I had already done it.

"I still think you should let the boys wear leather. It could be cool. Kind of a *'Grease'* wedding with them in their leather and us wearing pink." I look at Lips for like the twelfth time.

"My wedding is not going to be an Olivia-Newton-John musical. Not to mention, Dragon is a million times fucking cooler than John Travolta."

"True dat," Nikki chimes in. "Besides, it took me way too fucking long to convince Freak to wear a suit."

"How did you convince him?" Dani asks. She's sitting alone, holding herself away from us. It's a bad sign. One that means I have a very limited time frame in which to talk with her. All the girls except Nikki, who is on a round like pedestal at the moment, have been fitted. There's a lady going around putting pins in Nikki's dress, while we watch. I'm so ready for this fitting to be over. I would never admit it to Dragon, but I'm starting to regret demanding a big wedding. I don't even know why I did. I just wanted something big to mark my marriage to him. It might be a fucked up fairytale, but it was *my* fairytale and I wanted it to be celebrated. I was stupid. I should have dragged Dragon's ass to Gatlinburg, Tennessee, found a chapel, married him and been done with it. Every day that we get closer to our wedding my panic increases. I have this fear that I never will get my happily ever after.

"I threatened to tell the world what his real name was," Nikki says bringing my head back around to the conversation.

"I figured it was blow jobs, that's how I did it with Dragon."

The woman pinning Nikki's dress looks up and blushes, then buries her face in the pink satin. I look over at Dani, she half-way smiles. It's something.

"Oh, that probably didn't hurt." Nikki agrees. "Well

that, and the private party we had with Crush."

"Fuck me! You little hooker!" Lips responds.

Nikki flips her off. "Like you haven't taken a ride on the Crush train."

"Not in a long time. Six is not a sharer."

"Sucks for you." Nikki pipes up.

"Not so much. Six knows how to work it. Can't deny it though, Crush did some magic shit."

"Girl, you don't lie."

I'm looking over at Dani and notice the conversation has grabbed her attention. It surprises me to see the distaste on her face. I know for a fact that since Dani has broken away from Michael, she has no problem having threesomes, or what-the-heck-ever else. I don't understand it exactly; it doesn't jive with the young Dani I met. Still, it's further proof that the Dani that survived Michael is not the Dani that I once knew. He took everything from her, most notably her innocence.

I notice the girl that is pinning Nikki's dress is blushing like crazy. The boys of the Savage MC would eat her alive, it would probably be the best thing that could happen to her. Maybe I should introduce her to Frog? That boy needs a new name. I don't understand most of the names the boys have. Dragon, of course, but the others leave me shaking my head. He told me once that Dancer got his name because he used to be a big street boxer. I shudder to think how Frog got his.

"I need a drink," Dani speaks up, rising off of the chair, in the corner, she's been brooding in.

"Sounds good girl, but if I don't get back, Six will send out a search party."

LOVING NICOLE

"Freak too," Nikki adds, "we're supposed to go to Tennessee today to pick up some shit that the boys ordered."

"I'm out of here," Dani says already heading to the door.

"I think I'll join Dani. Lips, can you have Crusher come back and pick us up?"

"Yeah, where'd he go?" She asks.

"He said something about all the dresses and pink was making his cock fall off," Nikki says.

"Can't have that."

"Girl, you ain't lying," I hear Nikki agree before I run to catch up with Dani, who just went out the door.

"Hold up, Dani!" I grumble.

She stops on the sidewalk and turns to look at me.

"Dragon will flip if you don't show up with the other women."

"We need to talk."

"I'm getting a drink."

"Then we'll talk over drinks."

Dani gives me the what-the-fuck-are-you-talking-about look and motions at my stomach.

I roll my eyes.

"I'll have chocolate milk."

Dani looks up at the sky. "This is what my life has come to. We'll go to Weavers, I doubt the Den or Pussy's even has chocolate milk."

I grin, "Hey girls, tell Crush to pick us up at Weavers," I yell back through the door of the shop, then reclose it and wrap my hand around Dani's. We walk down the street and, if the shadow of Michael wasn't over us, I

35

would love every minute of it.

"You okay?"

"Not really," Dani responds honestly.

I don't say anything. What could I say? I totally relate. We walk the rest of the way in silence. When we make it to Weaver's, we take a seat at one of the tables outside. A waitress comes and takes our orders. I order a foot long hot dog and a large chocolate milk. This is what baby Dragon has reduced me to. I smile. It's *awesome*.

Dani orders a diet soda. It drives me crazy. The woman is like a size four, maybe smaller by this time, because she keeps losing weight. If I was as skinny as her ass, I'd live on nothing but doughnuts and chocolate.

We're quiet. Dani is running her finger over the Styrofoam cup of her drink, deep in thought. I'm afraid to get into it. The waitress brings my hotdog and I smile at her. When she leaves, I decide to dig in—in all ways.

I grab the hotdog, ignoring the way the chili drops on my hands as I take a bite. I put it down, wiping my hands off while I chew.

"No more notes?"

"No."

Well this conversation is going nowhere fast.

"We need to tell Dragon."

"No. We. Do. *Not*."

"Yes, we *do*. He needs to know there could be trouble on his doorstep soon. He can't protect us, if he doesn't know."

"He can't protect us anyway," Dani argues.

"Yes, he can."

"No, he can't."

"Damn it, Dani. Dragon needs to be prepared. There's too much to lose."

"I know that, Nic. Don't you think I know that? Fuck. Don't you get that I live daily with all the losses I've had since I met Michael Kavanagh?"

"Dani…I don't mean…"

"I *know* what you mean, Nic. Fuck, I *know* what I've cost you. I do. I wake up with nightmares about it. That's *why* I want to leave now. To protect you and little Dragon. Fuck, even to protect Dragon. I don't want any of you to get hurt. Michael is my problem. You guys didn't choose this."

"You didn't exactly choose it either, Dani." I defend because she didn't. Even the fucked up choices that she's made, I couldn't say I wouldn't have made the exact same ones. Hell, maybe even worse ones.

"I made the choice to bring you into them. I shouldn't have."

"Fuck that. You couldn't do it on your own."

"I could have, I was weak. I should have fought to keep you safe."

"Afternoon, ladies."

My head jerks around to see an older man standing by our table. He's stocky, not overweight really, it's more like muscles that have been neglected over the years. His hair is gray. Something about him sends off warning bells.

"Not interested, buddy. Move along," Dani says. Perhaps she doesn't get the same vibe from him, I'm not sure. She barely glances at him.

"Really, *Mrs.* Kavanagh, I assumed *you* would be most interested in what I have to say."

My heart stops. My eyes lock onto Dani's. I watch as the color slowly drains from her face.

"Sorry, you have the wrong person," I say, reaching under the table to put my hand on Dani's leg. Her hand meets mine under the table and grips it tight.

"Oh, I don't believe I do at all, Ms. Wentworth."

"That's *Mrs.* West."

"That's not quite true. At least not yet."

"Who the hell are you?" I tear my eyes away from Dani and look at the stranger. He's too damn smug and condescending to suit me.

"That's neither here nor there right now. I have a message for you, Melinda. It's from your husband."

"I…I don't…."

"Save it, we both know that you would be lying. Mr. Kavanagh will be in town next week. He will expect you at this address on the day and time listed. Do *not* disappoint him," he says putting a piece of paper on the table.

Dani looks at it and then back up at the stranger. Slowly, her back stiffens and the fear that had been dogging her since she got the reminder of her past life disappears. She meets his eyes, her face is cold and not an ounce of the fear she is truly feeling shows. Her hands cross under her breasts and she gives off the badass vibe that she has adopted since she first ran to me years ago.

"You can tell Mr. Kavanagh to go fuck himself—preferably with a sawed-off shotgun and the safety in the off position."

The man looks at her and you can see the disdain in his eyes and the way he regards her. I want to strike out at him, but I don't. Doing so will only make a bad situation worse.

"I can see hiding in the hills with a bunch of unedu-cated Neanderthals has had an unfortunate effect on you, Mrs. Kavanagh. A shame but, hopefully, not an irrevoca-ble change."

"Being around real people has had a fucking great effect on me, douche bag. Why don't you get the fuck out of here so I can enjoy my dinner? I got to tell you, your stink is starting to affect my appetite."

"Really, Mrs. Kavanagh, I do hope you remember who you are before you meet with your husband."

Dani flips him off with both fingers and the man's face colors as the other customers take notice because, well, Dani is *not* being quiet.

"I would suggest you remember your station before coming to your husband."

"I would suggest you go to hell."

"Do not make Mr. Kavanagh come and get you. Rest assured your punishment will be much worse if you do. You have brought enough disgrace upon the Kavanagh name."

Dani and I remain quiet as we watch the asshole walk off. I hear Dani let out a breath and move my head to watch her. It's then I see the tell-tale trembling in her hands and the over-bright sheen in her eyes.

"I'm going to have to leave, Nic."

I nod. She can't stay—not now.

"I know. I'll help you relocate and we'll…"

"No."

"Dani, I can…"

"You can't be part of it. I will not be responsible for

you getting hurt anymore."

"Dani, we've been over this."

"We have, so you should understand. It's time I stand on my own two feet."

"We need to talk about…."

"No, at least not right now. Here come's Crusher. Let's just let it go for now. You get back to Dragon."

"What about you? Where are you going?"

"Think I'll head down to the Den and find someone to scratch an itch," she says and I'm probably the only person who can tell that the smile doesn't reach her eyes—not even a little bit.

"If you want company tonight Hell Cat, I'm free."

Dani leans back, her lips going into a full kiss-my-ass-kind-of-smirk.

"Hell Cat?"

"It seems to fit," he shrugs.

Dani shakes her head and gets up from the table.

"I don't think so, stud."

"Baby, I could scratch your itch so well you'd purr for days."

"From what I hear your scratcher has been around so much, it's liable to cause an itch a girl needs medicine for."

"Didn't realize I was dealing with Queen Elizabeth."

She stops and turns around and looks at him. I can't stop from watching them. In some ways they remind me of the way Dragon and I are with each other.

"What the hell are you talking about, Crusher?" She asks.

"The virgin queen?"

She shakes her head, "Long way from a virgin baby, I

just don't happen to want Nikki and Lips' sloppy seconds."

"I could make sure you liked it."

"Bigger men than you have tried and failed—and I do mean bigger," Dani says before turning around and walking away from us.

"See? Pussy with claws. Hell Cat," Crusher yells back and Dani flips him off, not bothering to turn around. If I wasn't so worried about her, I would have laughed.

Chapter 7

DRAGON

'M SITTING IN the club, with my woman in my lap. The place is mostly empty tonight. All the brothers have gone to the Den or Pussy's. In fact, besides me and Nicole, the only other ones around are Hawk, Frog and Nailer. They're playing cards with one of the new prospects. A few of the Twinkies are hanging around them. The mood in the club seems almost depressing. I can't remember it being like this except for right after we found out about Irish. I still don't understand his betrayal. It had to be about more than money, but I've tried for months and months to find out more—there just seems to be nothing to find. I try to pull my mind out of those dark thoughts, before they have time to settle too deep.

"You're awful quiet, Mama."

"Got a lot on my mind tonight," she whispers.

I reach down and grab her hand, bringing it to my lips, before locking our fingers together and pressing them against my chest.

"You've been quiet since you came back from the dress fitting. Talk to me."

"I just have a lot to think about. I'm okay, Dragon,"

she says. I hate this feeling in my gut that tells me my woman is not being completely truthful with me, so I try to tap it down. I don't really succeed.

"Someone has been stalking around the club."

I feel her stiffen up against me and the muscles in her hands contract.

"Stalking?"

"Hanging around outside the gates, filming. Visiting the club businesses. That kind of thing."

"Any idea who?" She asks and there's a tremor in her voice. Is it concern for the club or fear of something else? *Fuck.*

"Not really, no. We have a few leads."

"I see," she says and you can definitely hear the tremor in her voice.

"Anything you want to tell me, Mama?"

"Should there be?" She asks, curling into my side and burying her face into my shoulder. I can feel the moisture against my skin.

Something is bothering her and tearing her up. I need to fix it. I can't if she doesn't let me in. My hand curls into her hair holding her close. What did this? What brought us to the point where she's not trusting me? Was it something I did? Didn't do?

"You need to talk to me, Nicole. I know you have something going on. Talk to me about it so I can help."

"I think Dani's going to leave," she whispers.

A big part of me is pissed the fuck off that the woman is causing problems for my girl. I can't lie, there's even another part of me that is happy to see her leave. Still, if her leaving is what is wrong with Nicole, I need to try and stop that. I want my woman happy.

"Why?"

"She…she feels it'd be better for her to start over somewhere else. She…she feels guilty over…," she pauses as if trying to pick her words out carefully. "…She feels guilty over the choices she made."

I kiss the top of Nicole's head.

"Would it help if I talked to her?"

"No. I think it's probably for the best."

"She'll be here for the wedding baby, and you can still keep in touch with her," I say trying to make her feel better, and figuring I'm failing when her tears fall harder against my neck.

"No. She'll be leaving before the wedding."

"Who's leaving?"

I look up to give Crusher a pissed off glare, but he ignores it—like usual. Instead he sits down across from me and Nic.

"Have a seat," I grumble with sarcasm, which is completely lost on Crusher.

He flips me off and takes a swig of his beer. "So, who's leaving?"

"Dani," I tell him, holding Nic closer.

He looks at me and I can tell the news upsets him. He is not a happy motherfucker. I don't like it, for numerous reasons. Maybe it is good that Dani is leaving.

"Gonna take my woman to bed," I grumble, and stand up with Nicole still in my arms, my arm under her legs and my other arm around her upper body. She used to complain when I carted her around. She's given that up, thank fuck. I guess she realized it won't do her a bit of good, I love having her in my arms.

"Good enough. See ya' tomorrow, Boss-man."

I grunt my reply. I lay Nicole on our bed and go back and lock the door, returning to hold her close. I listen to her crying in the dark, letting her get it out of her system.

"Mama, is there something more going on with Dani?"

There's no immediate reply so I let the silence stretch out farther.

"Mama…"

"Dragon, she's leaving. Can't we just let it go at that? If she was staying, then maybe it would matter."

"I can help her…"

"I'm just going to miss her. She'll be safe."

Safe. That word punches me in the gut. I should question her farther, I should demand more information. I do neither of those. Maybe I'm just fucking tired of all the shit that's been coming at my family. I don't fucking know. So, I don't question it. I put my hand over my woman's stomach and feel my son kick and just remain quiet. It doesn't take long, twenty minutes at the most and my woman is sleeping. Her breathing evens out, she's got this cute little whistle that couldn't be called a snore and she curls into me.

I carefully get my pillow and pad it gently to her side so she can hug it, then I get up. I'm not sleeping, not with all this shit in my head. I leave the room with one last glance at my woman. I'm upset with her. Fuck yeah, I am. She should trust me enough to talk to me. I can't make her—which means I'm going to have to take matters into my own hands.

"Hey Drag, you're stirring late," Dancer says, as I make it to the main entrance of the club.

"Yeah. What are you doing here?" I ask, because it's not a secret that Dancer hates being around the club. Brother is doing better, but he still can't handle large crowds. On the times I've seen him with them, he keeps Red close.

"Carrie was craving some of Nicole's homemade strawberry dip. So she begged until I brought her ass here to raid the Club's fridge. So late now, I figure we'll stay here and go home in the morning."

"We've become pussy-whipped brother, wrapped around the fingers of two women. Never thought I'd fucking see the day."

Dance shrugs, "Can't answer for you, but no fucking place I'd rather be. It sure as hell is more than I deserve."

I nod, I can't argue. I feel the same.

"Glad to see you and Red are working through shit."

For a minute his eyes take on a glazed haunted look, but it's gone so quick I almost miss it.

"What's up with you anyway? Hardly ever see you around once Nicole goes to bed."

"That's because her body is a hell of a lot nicer to be around than your ugly ass, but fuck, you're never here, so what do you know?"

"Point made. Still?" He says, motioning with his drink.

I look at him, he's not drinking alcohol. Brother is drinking a damn Coke out of a can. He hasn't touched a drop since he got his woman back. He wasn't an alcoholic, but he said it was too tempting to lose himself in the bottle. He said it was much more enjoyable to lose himself in his woman. I have to agree, but I'm pouring myself a shot of Jack. Dance moves over and I stare at the drink I just poured.

"Some kind of shit is going down with Nic's girl, Dani."

"Fuck a duck."

"That about sums it up."

"Bad? Should I take Carrie and Nicole out of here?"

"Nah, at least I don't think so. Nicole would tell me if it was that serious. I get the feeling it might be some ex-boyfriend."

"Damn, that girl is fucked in the head when it comes to that shit."

"Apparently."

"Drag? You think it's cool?" He asks putting his empty can on the bar.

My finger is moving over the rim of my glass. Every part of me wants to say *fuck no*. At the same time, I know if Nicole knew something would endanger the club then she'd tell me. I trust my woman.

"Drag?" He asks standing up.

I down my drink and drop it on the bar.

"Yeah man, I'm sure."

"Sure about what?" Red asks coming out of the kitchen.

"Hey Red, you're looking good."

"Hey Dragon," she says in her quiet voice. She goes immediately to Dancer's side and curls into him. Dancer's hand comes automatically over her shoulder and he kisses the top of her head. "Sure about what?"

"Nothing, Care Bear. Just asking Dragon if he needed

my help with something."

"I don't, but if it changes, I'll hit you up."

Dance nods.

"You want to go home or stay here?"

Red holds up her container of dip that she got from the fridge, "Let's go home."

"Got what you came for?" Dance asks smiling down at her, and it feels good to see my brother happy.

"Oh yeah," Red says.

"What do you plan on eating that with? We don't have any strawberries in the house."

She looks up at him and blushes a darker red than her hair. Dance throws his head back and laughs. He *laughs*. Shit, I still find that unreal.

"Care Bear, one of these days you are so going to tell me what I want to hear without blushing."

"Jacob, hush." She mumbles as he takes her in his arms and hugs her. She peeks over his arm at me and I just shake my head.

"Catch you two on the flip side."

"You got it, brother," Dance says as they turn to leave.

"Take it easy on my brother Red, he's an old man you know."

"Fuck off, Dragon," he barks, giving me the one-fingered salute.

I laugh. I'm glad to see my brother doing so much better. We still have to get revenge for him. He asked me to hold up. He wants to do it himself, but says he's not ready. I've not pushed it. Seems I have enough fires to put out.

Once they leave, I lock the doors. Anyone else wants

in, they have keys. I'm starting to feel that burning in my gut all the time now. Fuck, I hope Nicole isn't holding out on me.

Chapter 8

NICOLE

"WHEN ARE YOU leaving?" I ask Dani. It's the next day, and we're sitting at one of the picnic tables outside the club compound.

It's a gorgeous summer day and with fall approaching soon, I want to enjoy it. My hand absently strokes my stomach. I do it a lot, but more so lately. Dani and I have a complex relationship, but it is close in ways no one but the two of us will ever understand. We've been through hell together. When I needed a friend and had no one, Dani was there. When she was actually trapped in hell, I helped to bring her out. Our secrets, our sadness bonded us together. So, the thought of bringing little Dragon into this world and not having Dani there to hold my hand, to be with me…it kills me. I can't tell her that but I know she feels it. I know that she is terrified to leave. I also know she doesn't have a choice now and that sucks. I hate Michael Kavanagh, despise him. I'd like to cut off his balls and deep fry… No, I want to deep fry his balls while they were still attached and then cut them off and feed them to him. That'd be infinitely better.

"Not sure. Soon though. Definitely way before my

supposed *meeting* with the hubby."

"Good plan. Hey, at least we got warning and he just didn't swoop in and grab us," I answer, trying to make light of it. I actually am surprised he didn't take Dani forcibly, before we had a heads up.

"It's his way. He likes to be dramatic and bigger than life."

"Yeah, well."

"I know…," she says sadly, looking up at the sky. "I'm going to miss Kentucky. When you suggested I move here to hideout I thought you were insane, but I've loved every minute of it. Hell, even Roy likes it."

"Will he be going with you?"

"No, he's settled here. He's actually met someone. My visit with him was an eye opener. I'd never seen him so happy."

"That's good, but I don't want you to be alone. Maybe we should tell Dragon and face this head on. I know…"

"Not going to happen, Nic. I've thought about it and this is the best for all concerned. Once I'm gone Michael will leave you guys alone, most notably you."

"Dani…"

She reaches over, grabs my hand and looks me in the eyes. I can see the moisture there, and the deep sadness. It hurts me. I wrap my hands around hers and squeeze tight.

"One of the best things that happened to me was meeting you at Three Oaks Academy."

"Dani…"

"I mean it, Nic. When you decided to bail out of that school and tell your parents to suck it, I was so in awe of you. I wanted that kind of courage. You've always seen me as the strong one, but it's you…it's always been you."

I swallow, but the words I want to use to respond are frozen in my throat. Clogged up with emotion so deep, I'm afraid to let it out. I forget, years of living our lie has made it an alternate reality and I just go with it. It's completely untrue, this history I allow Dragon and everyone to believe. My history with Dani is much more twisted and confusing. I didn't meet Dani in Kentucky, we didn't grow up together. We didn't go to school together, unless you count the month in hell my parents made me try out TOA (Three Oaks Academy), husband shopping. None of my carefully laid past is true, save one. Dani has and always will be my best friend, and a person who owns a large part of my heart.

"Dani, you're strong, most women would have never survived what you did."

"It was weak to ask you for help. It was weak to drag Roy into it."

"No it wasn't. Family means being there for each other. If you don't tell Roy that you're leaving, you will hurt him."

"Roy broke me out of the prison I was in. He put his life on the line to get me out of New York. He helped me set up a new identity and kept me safe. I think Roy has done enough."

"He won't see it like that."

Dani shrugs, "He won't know."

"Damn it, Dani."

"Just let it go Nic, it's time I stand on my own. There's no choice really. You have Dragon and little Dragon to think of. Roy has his new boyfriend and a settled life in

Kentucky. I can't stay here. You know what will happen if I do."

"I…Will I hear from you again?"

"I'll get a message to you somehow—when I know it's safe."

I nod. I'm not happy, but I know it's all I will get.

"What about money?"

"I still have all that money Roy and I took out of Michael's wall-safe, so I'm pretty much set for life. I just don't like touching it. I'll use it to get relocated and buy some new documents. I'll be fine."

"I want to be able to send you pictures of the baby…"

"We'll figure it out. I want to see little Dragon, too.

"I know your mind is made up, but I wish you'd let me get Dragon involved."

"You're starting to sound like a broken record," Dani says and I want to argue further but I hear the door open behind me. I look up and see Crusher coming out of the main entrance. I can't help but notice the way he's looking at Dani; his eyes never leave her. I doubt he even notices I'm sitting here.

"Please tell me you didn't go there, Dani."

"Go where?" She asks, acting like she's clueless. She's sitting sideways on the bench facing me, but she keeps looking to her side at Crusher.

"Crusher?" I prompt.

"I had an itch."

"They make shit for that, it's called flea spray."

She looks up at me and for a second, a small space in time, I see my old friend, the one I met years ago when I tried to do as my parents insisted. Then with a flash, she is gone. It happens sometimes, I see her the girl I loved and who loved me—freely. The girl who had yet to be chewed up and spit out by the world. God, I miss her.

"This was more fun."

"He's not one of your boy toys, Dani. Crusher might seem laid back and easy going, but…"

"Spare me Nic, at this point, I think it's safe to say I'm more familiar with Crusher than you are."

"And you're still going to do this?"

"Tonight, anyway."

"Dani…"

"My vibrator batteries are dead, sometimes a girl has to do what a girl has to do." With that she walks off towards Crusher.

I do not see good things coming from this, but I'm too damn worried about everything else to think about it for now.

Chapter 9

DRAGON

THIS HAS TO be one of the best ideas I've had. I watch as my woman and Red are lying on lounge chairs looking over the lake. I decided it was time to get the family together. We're having a big picnic and bonfire at the Twin Rocks picnic shelter and camping area, overlooking Laurel Lake. Red and Nicole are resting, the men are scattered around talking to a couple of the Twinkies that came, or shooting the breeze with each other. Dance and I are manning the grill. Heck, even Bull came. He's kind of quiet and off to himself still, but I saw Frog and Hawk go over to join him. It's a perfect, relaxing day. The only thing I'm finding troubling is the way Crusher and Dani are sitting in the sand talking to each other. You'd be stupid not to see what's going on.

I know it's because of everything that went down with Nicole and her getting shot. I should let it go like my woman asked, but I can't. I almost lost Nicole. Maybe it is unfair, but there-the-fuck-it-is. I look at Dani and I feel anger. So, I'm not exactly filled with good vibes watching my brother fall for her.

"That looks like trouble," Dance says, echoing my

thoughts.

"Pretty much," I agree, taking a sip of my beer.

"Carrie says Dani's leaving?"

"Yeah."

"Think it has to do with the shit Freak found on the tapes?"

"Probably, fuck if I know. Neither her nor Nicole are talking."

"Should we step in?"

"Who the hell knows? I…"

Where once the area was filled with talking and laughter, now there's screaming as gunfire erupts around us. Dancer and I take off running at the same time to cover our women. I see out of the corner of my eye that Crusher is doing the same with Dani. I'm useless in helping the other members scramble. I pull Nicole off the chair, trying to be gentle. I flip the chair to its side. It won't stop a bullet, but it might mess up the aim of the shooter. I keep my woman covered as much as I can, even though she's begging me to protect myself. Fucking woman has zero survival skills when it comes to taking care of her own hide.

As quick as the gunfire begins it stops, when Freak and the other brothers start firing back. I look over the top of the chair, trying to get my bearings. I focus on an old black Ford truck peeling out of the parking lot.

"Hold up!" I shout. Slowly the brothers stop shooting. "Follow those fuckers. If they get away I'm going to make sure heads roll!" I stand, helping Nicole to her feet. "Mama, I'm going to go find out who the fuck that was. Are you okay? The baby?"

"We're fine, Dragon," she whispers shakily, the side of her face covered with sand and there are tears in her eyes. I bend down and kiss her hard, taking her taste inside of me, because I need it. She's my air. The reason I live.

"Bull, protect the women and get them back to the compound."

"Yeah, alright Drag," Bull says, but something in his tone grabs me. I don't have time to address it. "Dance, Crush, you're with me."

I'M FUCKING TIRED. It's been hours. We followed the fuckers and found the truck abandoned at the base of one of the hiking trails through the Daniel Boone National Forest. Crush and I managed to grab one of the fuckers, but the other one or two (I can't even be sure how fucking many there were) managed to get away.

We brought weasel back to the cabin for interrogation. It didn't take long. He sang like a fucking canary. Weak-ass, sniveling son of a bitch. I would probably have been doing him a favor if I had ended him, but I didn't. We have plans for him.

I slam into the front doors of the compound and I'm pissed for many reasons. Bull looks up at me and his face goes tight.

"What's up?"

"Crush and Dance will fill you in. Where's my woman?"

"She was feeling bad, went to lay down."

"Thanks, man. Church meeting in two hours."

Bull nods, and I'm preoccupied, but I see something flash in his eyes. I should stop and ask what the fuck is going on, but I can't. I put it on my list. I know Bull is dealing with shit. His voice is ragged and hoarse, he has a scar on his neck and his body is weaker. Rehab helped some, but he's having issues. I need to be there for him, but I just don't have the time right now. I put it on the back burner and go to find my woman.

She's lying on the bed, but she's not asleep. She's wide awake, staring at the door, with those same damn tears in her eyes.

"Mama, we need to talk," I close the door behind me and lean on it, waiting.

"I don't think we do. It's done now."

"Done? Nicole, what the fuck are you talking about? It's not done. I've just spent the last hour interrogating some jerk to find out that there's a freaking lunatic out there gunning for *my* woman *and* Dani, because it seems *Dani* was married to the fucker and ran out on him fucking five years ago! How do I not know this, Nicole? How could *you* not tell me about *this*?"

"Wasn't my secret to tell, Dani has a right to her privacy, Dragon—even from you," she says getting up.

"She is married, Nicole. To a rich-ass lunatic who thought she was dead. She stole five hundred grand off of him. You had to *know* he'd never give up trying to find his damn money. You had to know he'd eventually *hunt you down* for answers!"

"He had no reason to. He had no idea that Dani and I were still in touch. We covered our bases damn good," she says calmly. I swear if the woman didn't own my soul I would be tempted to slap some sense into her.

Covered their bases? What the fuck? She's an amateur trying to take on the big boys. I had Freak research this Michael Kavanagh. What I found out still fucking leaves me with chills just thinking what someone like that would do to Nicole. I don't want my woman anywhere around this fucker. I do not want her in his line of fire.

I look at her like I have no idea who she is, because honest to God, I don't right now.

"Well guess what Nicole, it appears he plays connect the fucking dots pretty damn good because he found not only *Dani*, he's found *you* and the *club*, too. All because you and Dani were too stupid to give me a heads up."

She steps back like I slapped her. I realize I didn't say it right, but I'm fucking pissed. I step away from the door and come closer to her.

"Damn it, you should have told me! We're supposed to share this shit, we're a team."

"Don't you pull that crap, Dragon. There's a whole shitload of stuff you don't share with me."

"Club business only—I have to keep that between me and the boys. You've been around long enough to know how that goes. Don't start crying about it now, just because *you fucked up.*"

I know that's a fucked up way to put it. Shit. I can tell by the way her blue eyes glitter with so much anger that this is going from bad to worse in a hurry. I just can't get a handle on it. She's left me feeling betrayed. Still, the look in her eyes hurts me. Has my woman ever looked at me like that?

"Club business. How fucking convenient. Newsflash Dragon, Dani is *my girl* and *our* business is just that, *our* business. I didn't fuck up shit, you're just being a self-righteous prick."

"We're having a baby. We're getting married in a few fucking days and you say this crap to me?"

"Yeah, well I don't see that happening."

"The fuck you say, woman, I've about gone my limit with your ass."

"That's good Dragon, because I think I've done the same with yours." She growls as she stomps away from me.

"Where the hell are you going?"

"I need time away from you."

I watch as Nicole opens the door to our bedroom. Her words play over in my mind. Since the day we met, I don't think we've spent more than a complete day away from each other. I need her like air. Her words cut open a piece of me that I thought had been healed. The wound is even more intense because it is inflicted by my woman.

"Mama, don't do this. Whatever this is, we'll work it out, but don't take us to this place."

She turns around and we're only standing about three feet apart, but it feels like a fucking ocean.

I need time away from you.

"You don't get to decide this, Dragon. To say that I have to tell you everything when you aren't willing to do the same. You don't get that. It can't work that way."

"Your secrets almost got us killed today, Mama. They almost ended the life of our son."

Her hand goes to her stomach and she presses against her stomach, the ring I gave her glitters in the semi-dark room.

"And your secrets don't do the same?"

My mind goes back to the day on the mountain when she got shot.

"You *always* knew there was shit going on, I didn't keep you in the dark Nicole, even if I couldn't give you all the details."

"I was going to tell you," she whispers.

"When? After the fuck-wad already killed someone I care about? Or worse, you? Do you know what the fuck it would do to me if I lost you?"

"I promised Dani I would wait until she left."

"Left? She can't leave, Nicole. This fucker will grab her the minute she tries to run. It's too late for that baby, and hell, as much as she pisses me the fuck off, I like the bitch. She's not facing this shit on her own."

"It's too late," she whispers and her hands go around her stomach cradling it as her tears fall harder. I'm getting fucking tired of seeing those tears fall from her eyes all the time.

"What do you mean it's too late? I got this, Mama. You know I'll always protect me and mine. Dani's your girl. That makes her part of the family. I won't let this Kavanagh fuck get her."

"She's gone, Dragon."

"What? What do you...?"

"She left not long after we got back. She's been planning it for days."

"Sit down on the bed Mama, I think it's time you and I talk this out," I say, uneasiness grabbing me at the idea of Dani out there alone.

Chapter 10

NICOLE

I SIT ON the bed and lift my head when I feel Dragon at my feet. He slides my sandals off, placing a kiss on each ankle once it's done. His touch is so gentle and completely at odds with the argument we've just had. I watch as he slowly trails his hands up my legs, pushing my dress up as he goes.

"What are you doing?"

"Getting you undressed for your nap," he says kissing a path up my leg.

"We...I thought we were fighting?"

"We're having words Nicole. I might be pissed, and you might be pissed but, Mama, get this straight...You're *my* woman and there is *no ending this*, or *time away* from us. You feel me?"

My heart stutters. I didn't mean the words when I said them. I'm scared, worn out, and terrified for Dani. I shouldn't have laid into Dragon like I did. I might be pissed off because it seems like a double standard, but in truth, I don't even disagree with him.

"I feel you," I whisper as his hands reach under my dress and pull down my panties. I shift so he can take them off. He throws them to the corner once they clear my legs.

He raises up and reaches out his hands to me, "Stand up, Mama."

I let his hands envelop mine and he pulls me up. My eyes stay locked on his as he slides the straps of my dress off my shoulders, and further still, until it pools at my feet.

"You're fucking beautiful, Mama."

"I'm as big as a house," I argue and being over six months pregnant, it's totally true. The only thing saving me from looking like a blimp in my wedding dress is the forgiving layers the designer fixed around the waist.

He bends down and flattens his tongue out against one of my nipples, licking it and then sucking it into his mouth. My head goes back as I moan. He slowly releases and does the next one the same way.

"Turn around."

His words shock and excite me. Since Dragon found out I was pregnant he has always been so careful with me. During sex, he makes sure I am in a positon where he controls the intensity of everything. Don't get me wrong, anyway we make love is good, but there are times I miss the down and dirty Dragon I fell in love with.

I do as he orders and my body shudders when his hands move up my breasts and pulls so my back is tight against him.

"Spread your legs out to make room for me Mama and bend over on the bed slowly," he whispers in my ear, his hot breath sending goosebumps over my skin.

I swallow, so fucking turned on I can feel the wetness gathering between my legs. I do as he says and smile when he reaches around and drags two pillows under me. I lean on them so I'm higher than the bed will allow and it makes it infinitely easier for me. The bed is tall, but as big as I am, it's hard to bend over these days.

His hand slides along my ass, his fingers pushing between the cheeks, teasing my opening. I bite my lip to keep from crying out in excitement. It seems like forever since he's played with me this way. His fingers move farther down sliding between the lips of my pussy, playing and exploring but never entering inside of me. One finger grazes over my clit before going back to play in the creamy wetness he has created.

"Fuck Mama, you're soaked for me. You need my cock?"

"Always. I need you to fuck me."

He tortures my clit and then goes back and plays with more of my juices. It's a sweet, torturing refrain that has me on the verge of climaxing in minutes.

"Who owns this pussy, Nicole?" He growls, continuing his movements in slow, methodical thrusts that have me ready to scream. When I push my ass against him he stills it by taking his other hand and clamping down on my side.

"You do, Dragon. It's yours. I'm yours," I acknowledge, as finally he slides two fingers inside of me, not going as deep as I want him to, but still it's more than he has allowed.

"Who owns your fucking body, Nicole?"

"You do. I told you, I'm yours." I whimper half out of my mind.

His thumb moves out to push on my clit while his

fingers tease inside of me, stretching my opening. He keeps thrusting them in and out, giving me a taste of what my body is craving, but never going deep enough to fully satisfy.

"You think you can live without my touch, Mama? You think this body can go without me?"

"No, I... fuck, Dragon, it was stupid. I shouldn't have said it. I love you sweetheart, I couldn't live without you. Please... Oh fuck!" I growl out when I feel his free hand come down and smack my ass hard while his fingers are still inside of me.

"We will never be done, Nicole," he growls, smacking my ass again this time with the hand that was in my pussy. The sticky wetness slides against the heat of the last blow. It feels so fucking good. He knows I love it when he plays me like this.

"Dragon...sweetheart...," my voice is dark and full of need.

"We are getting married, Nicole. You are wearing my fucking ring. You will keep wearing a cut that says you're my old lady and you will fucking be in my damned bed every fucking night, begging for my cock. You feel me, woman?" He orders, his hand connecting with my ass again.

I'm so wet it's sliding down my legs now. If he doesn't give me his cock soon, I'm going to come without him.

"Dragon...damn it..."

"We are forever, Mama, say it," he demands as once again, he delivers another blow.

The bite of pain and then the teasing he gives me after, work to send me into another zone and I can barely hold on.

"Yes," I cry out feeling the fluttering of my inner walls, so close to an orgasm. *So close.*

"Say it, Mama!" He growls again and I can hear the sound of his zipper sliding down behind me.

"Forever Dragon, we're forever."

He grunts in agreement, then all at once he's on the bed—naked, gloriously naked. He's lying down and pulls me on top of him. I straddle him immediately, even as I wish he had taken me like we were.

"*Dragon.*"

"Shh…Mama, grab my cock and take me inside. I love when you ride me."

"But, I want you like we were."

"Just take me until it feels good, Mama. Give me this. I love seeing you riding me, your hair sliding against your skin, your body swollen with my baby. Fuck, you have no idea, woman."

"I'm huge," I protest, but give in. I slide down on his cock because, even though I may want the other position, I will never pass on having Dragon inside of me.

He reaches up and pinches one of my swollen nipples in punishment. I cry out as the pain runs through me. His hands move to palm each side of my stomach, where he strokes it gently, his eyes are glued there, seemingly enraptured. Slowly he looks up and his eyes hold mine. The inky chocolate depths are so deep, I lose myself.

"I've never seen anything more beautiful in my fucking life, Nicole. Never."

I close my eyes and replay his words. My man. God, this man has a way of shattering whatever self-doubt I have and making me feel like I am the most beautiful woman in the world. He manages to heal the wounds left by my parents and numerous other idiots that have passed through in my life, and I don't even think he *tries*. He just does it. He believes it, believes in me. He makes *me* believe it, too.

Those are the last thoughts I manage to grasp before I pick up speed in my ride and focus on doing nothing but bringing us pleasure. He grips my hips, helping to support me as I slide down on his cock, over and over, doing my best to clench tight around him.

"That's it, Mama. Give it to me."

I can't maneuver like I once did; I am not flexible, nor agile. I've worried that Dragon would notice the difference and miss it. I worried for no reason. I see that in the look in his eyes, the way his hands move over my body, and more importantly, by the way my climax triggers his. I fracture into a million pieces, pleasure rocking me to my core, but he is right there with me. I hear him call out my name and feel his release.

Minutes later I'm lying on my side. Dragon has fixed it so we're now at the head of the bed and I'm using his chest as my pillow. It's still early in the evening, too early to be in bed, I guess. I don't care.

"Tell me about Dani, Mama," Dragon says and I wish I didn't have to.

"She's not from Kentucky and we didn't go to high school together."

Dragon's body tightens against mine and I feel shame for lying to him. He doesn't say anything though and he doesn't push me away, so I soldier on.

"I told you my parents insisted I go to college to find a suitable husband, but I refused; though not at first. I went for one semester. They sent me to Three Oaks Academy in Maryland. It was *the* premiere private college where trophy wives-in-training go."

Dragon kisses the top of my head and squeezes me to him. I take this as a good sign.

"That's where I sort of met Dani."

"Sort of?"

"Dani is a name she picked out of a Red Hot Chili Pepper's song. Her real name is Melinda Marinetti."

"Fuck me…"

"Of the Marinetti shipping…"

"I know the name, Nicole," Dragon replies and his voice is not happy. I take a breath and dive back in.

"Her father had just died. She had no one but him since her mom died when Dani was…"

"Melinda."

"She's Dani to me, she always will be," I try to explain and I can hear how upset he is, but I figure at this point in for penny, in for a pound—or whatever. "Anyways, when the will was read her father made it a stipulation that Dani would marry Michael or she would not inherit anything."

"Jesus."

"Pretty much. Michael was nice to Dani. He held her hand through the funeral, helped make the arrangements, and became her support system in a way. She thought he was perfect."

"He wasn't?"

"He wasn't happy she came to school. The will stipulated that Dani finish so many hours of college and other weird shit though, so he didn't stop her. After they married, that's when he changed."

"Changed?"

"Controlling, beatings…and more, but those things are Dani's alone to know, Dragon."

"Why didn't she leave?"

"Hard to leave a man who has that much power. She was young, terrified. There were a lot of reasons."

"She reached out to you?"

"I hated Three Oaks, one semester was all I could handle. I came back home and moved in with Roy's parents."

"Roy?" Dragon asks and his voice takes on that extra-growly texture to it.

"Cool your jets, sweetheart. Roy is like a brother to me and gay—very happily gay."

"Dani's brother?"

"He's not actually. We met him in Maryland and just clicked, though he and Dani have always been super close. When things got really bad Dani had nowhere else to go, she called me and Roy arranged to go get her. He was dating a man who could help her start a new life. With his help, Melinda died and Danielle Grant was born."

Dragon had shifted where he was on his side while we talked. When I finished he rolled over on his back and stared up at the ceiling. I lie there, not talking. Even remembering this story, totally glossing over the ugliness, exhausts me. I've told Dragon, but he has no idea, really. He couldn't. Dragon isn't a man who would ever hurt a woman—let alone hurt her in ways she'd never recover from and take joy from it.

"This is a fucked up mess, Mama."

"Yeah."

"You should have come to me. You should have trusted me with this so I could protect you and Dani."

His words hurt, I knew, of course, how he'd feel, but hearing it spoken out-loud and in his voice, a voice I love, *wounds me*. I shift to my side and prop my head on my arm. I would have liked to roll over on top of him, but our child prevents me. Instead, I take my free hand and exert enough pressure on the side of his face that he turns and looks at me. My thumb grazes over his strong chin. I try to will everything I feel for this man into my eyes. I want him to see how much I truly love him. I know I've done damage by keeping Dani's secrets, but it's important he sees it has hurt me too.

"Dragon, I love Dani. Until you and your club, she was the only family I ever had. I kept her secrets out of loyalty, because she asked me."

"Nicole…"

"But even after I agreed to keep them Dragon, I was still planning on telling you. I just couldn't right away. Dani has had so much betrayal. If I had betrayed her, I don't think she would have survived."

"Damn it. Mama, I can't keep you safe if you don't tell me. I can't keep her safe! Nicole, she's out there alone with no protection. That is *not* alright. You needed to let me in and trust that I can handle this shit."

"I do! It's not about if I trusted you. It never was! Dani didn't want you involved. She didn't want the club involved. You keep preaching, club business is club business. How you need to keep me safe. You should understand more than anyone that Dani felt this was *her* business, and she wanted to try and keep us all safe."

"Running away won't do it though. This psycho won't stop until he has Dani, and now that he knows she's been alive all this time and living off his money? He'll want revenge and he'll want it ugly."

My stomach clenches and this sick feeling explodes inside of me. Realistically, he's only telling me the truth, but I was trying to pretend differently.

"Maybe Dani's right and now that she's left, he'll give up. Maybe he'll grow tired when he can't find her."

"No, he'll find her and he'll use any means to achieve that."

"What do we do?' I whisper, because I know I was stupidly convincing myself that Dani was right. Hearing Dragon and the certainty in his voice, I'm terrified.

"Call your girl and get her to come home."

"I can't."

"Why can't you…"

"She said it was safer if I didn't know anything. She's going to contact me once she gets settled, through a prepaid phone she purchased when we were in town for the fitting. There's nothing I can do until then."

Dragon sighs, turning his head away from me and stares back at the ceiling.

"Then we wait, Mama. It's all we can do." The words echo into the heavy silence that has filled the room. They do nothing to assuage the fear that has taken root inside of me and the dark truth that echoes in my mind. By trying to protect my relationship and loyalty to Dani, I may have only succeeded in hurting her, or worse, getting her killed....

"Dragon," I break off in a cry of anguish as the tears over this whole thing finally break to the surface.

Sobs rack my body as Dragon pulls himself up into a sitting a position. He props himself up against the headboard for support, then drags me over into his lap and holds me close, petting my back, while adjusting the covers over our body. He soothes me, but the tears keep coming. Dragon kisses the top of my head and lets me cry.

"We'll find her Mama, we'll find her and figure all this out. I promise."

I try to hold onto those words, through my tears.

I really try.

Chapter 11

DRAGON

I HOLD NICOLE until she cries it out. Eventually exhaustion takes her over and she sleeps. I will *not* be sleeping. Fuck, after my woman talking like she was leaving me, I may never sleep again. At thirty-six years old, I don't think anything or anyone has ever gutted me like hearing Nicole tell me she needed time away from me.

I get her settled and she snuggles up against the pillow. I get dressed because I need a drink. *Fuck*, I need a drink. First, I called the church meeting. I'm running late, but what-the-fuck-ever at this point. Today has been one shit-storm after another.

"Does your woman know where Dani is?"

I barely make it out the door when Crusher comes at me. I reach out my hand and push his shoulder back. What the fuck?

"Nicole is sleeping fucker, step back into the main room and we'll talk."

"Fuck, that. I need to find Dani. Does your woman fucking know where she is or not?"

Crush's face is red, his hair is rumpled and the brother looks torn up. How did Dani get her hooks in him that deep, before I realized it?

"You need to step the fuck back, man. I told you Nicole is sleeping. She cried herself to sleep and by God she's going to rest. You feel me?"

Crush rakes his hands through his hair.

"You don't understand Drag, this bastard will hurt her."

Somehow, I just know the *her* he's talking about, is *not* Nicole. Probably, because I'm not stupid.

"You knew about this shit?" I growl walking through the hallway towards my office where we're meeting.

"I knew she was running. Didn't know what from, until all this shit went down. She left me a damn note, a fucking note!"

"Something you want to tell me, brother?" I ask as we close the door to the office. The others are already there.

"She's mine, Dragon. I've got to find her and you can either help me or get the fuck out of my way," Crush says and the room goes deathly quiet.

"You need to calm your ass and sit the fuck down," I say quietly. It's taking all I have right now not to lay my brother out.

"Bullshit! If Nicole were involved, you'd be tearing the place apart trying to find this motherfucker!" Crush argues.

I grab him by his cut and slam him back against the wall. His hands come up but he doesn't fight me. Still, I can see the need to do so in his eyes.

"Nicole is involved, motherfucker. Now you need to listen to me. Step. The. Fuck. Down. Do *not* cause me more shit, because all that will do is slow us down."

He stares at me, his body is rigid.

"I will find her, Dragon."

"No, Crush, *we'll* find her. Last thing you need to do is go off half-cocked and take on this dude. He's a bad motherfucker and he has the money to back that shit up. We'll handle this my way. You feel me?"

He shrugs away from my hold, I let him. I'd like to acquaint his teeth with my fist for mouthing off to me, but I've got bigger fish to fry.

"Freak, you got my info?" I growl turning back to the table where the rest of the men are sitting. For now, I'm letting Crusher slide. One thing is clear though, his head is not in the game. I'm going to have to be careful how I deal with him. Part of me understands it, hell I've been there with Nicole. Still, you got to keep your head at all times. If you don't your woman ends up dead and maybe a lot more along with her.

"Yeah, man," he replies sliding over a manila folder towards me. I pick it up off the table and look through the information he's gathered on Michael Kavanagh. I thumb through the papers while sitting down.

"Where's our guest?"

"Frog's sitting on him at the shed," Hawk speaks up.

I look up at all my brothers. None are smiling, which is good because we're in the middle of a crap-fest. That said, Bull's look is different. Fuck, I can't deal with more than one fucking mess at a time.

"Call Frog, tell him to let the son of a bitch go."

"The fuck you will, that might be the only lead we have back to Dani!" Crusher yells.

"Crush, man, I'm not telling your ass again. Rein your

shit in. Nicole said Dani left on her own. She promised to check in soon with Nicole. We'll have to wait to handle that shit then. For now, listen up because I'm not going to fucking explain myself to you again. We're letting the weasel go and we're following him back to his man. Got it?"

"We need to work him over and find out exactly what they know about Dani. We can get this Michael's whereabouts from him that way. None of this cat and mouse shit," Crusher argues yet-a-fuck-again.

If I were still standing up, I'd kick his ass. I'm too fucking tired and worn out to fool with it right now.

"Get the fuck out!" I order instead. The room goes silent.

"Damn it, Drag! We have to…"

"You're not hearing me motherfucker, I said get the fuck out. I can't deal with your shit right now. You are out of this until you manage to get your head out of your ass, untie the knot in your balls and listen to sense."

"Drag!"

"Get out, motherfucker! *Now.*"

Crusher's face is frozen and he's pissed. I can see it big time, I also know I'm doing this now, so there's not a bigger problem later.

He slams out the door without another word.

I sigh heavily. *Fuck.*

"Now, let's talk over this shit and then you call Frog and tell him to let the son of a bitch free."

Chapter 12

CRUSHER

I STOMP OUT of the meeting without another fucking word. Son of a bitch wouldn't listen anyways. He'd be singing a different tune if it was Nicole out there missing. I've been messing around with Dani for a month now. I thought it was just sex. Hell, that's all I've ever wanted from a woman. I don't think I'm built for more—or at least I wasn't.

Then the damn woman turned shit on me. She got jealous of a fucking night I had before her and I even hooked up. Freak's woman Nikki had never had a threesome and wanted to. Brother trusted me to show his woman a good time—and it fucking was a *good* time. Still, it wasn't something I was looking to repeat. Dani flipped her fucking lid. Sure, she thought it was something more recent, but still. If I live to be a hundred I don't think I will ever figure that damned woman out.

Maybe that's what keeps me interested. I don't know. All I know, is that she is different from any woman I've been with. Dani has so many layers, I'm not sure I'll ever reach the center. The only thing I am certain of is that trying will be a hell of a ride.

The last few days have been special. Something happened when she thought I had screwed another woman while visiting her bed. I don't know what exactly, I just know it caused her to reveal a little more of herself to me and in doing that I saw this vulnerable side I never knew existed with Dani. She let me in…not a lot, but enough that she spoke vaguely of her past and her fears.

I need to keep her safe. She might not have told me the story, but I saw the desperation in her eyes when she thought of it. I heard the fear in her voice and the hopelessness that was inside of her. I'm not in love; I don't *do* that shit. I will never be the type to be owned by a woman like Dragon, or Dance for that matter. But, I wasn't lying when I told Dragon she's mine. I've claimed her and I *will* protect her.

So even though it's against Dragon's orders, and everything I should do as a member of the club, I'm getting the ATV out of the shelter and driving up to the cabin. I'm going to interrogate the bastard and I *will* find out where the fuck this Michael is before he can hurt Dani.

"HEY CRUSH, DRAG and the boys didn't say anyone was coming back tonight," Frog says as he unlocks the shed door after I knock.

"Drag's stressed man, he probably forgot. He tell you about plans for the piss-ant we're holding?"

"Yeah dude, I was just about to go in there and let him go."

"I'll do it, I'm supposed to relieve you anyways. I got to play shadow and see where the fuck the dude heads out to."

"Sounds like a fun job—not."

"Pretty much, but one of the sorry-ass perks of being the club VP."

"I hear ya'. I guess I'm out of here then. Call me when you need relief."

"Will do," I say and barely keep from screaming *get the fuck out*. Frog pisses in the wind for another ten minutes or so and finally leaves.

I lock the door and go into the back area where the dipshit is chained up. There's no coming back from what I'm about to do. I know it, but I'm still going to do it. Am I doing it for Dani? Yeah, she's a big reason but not all of it. Dani screams of fear, she screams of being trapped. She screams with the same scent and brokenness as another woman in my life. A woman I lost long ago. A woman I wasn't able to help and that won't be the case this time.

He looks up at me when I walk in. You can tell Dragon has worked him over pretty good; he's stripped naked and chained from the ceiling, hanging like a slab of meat. Still, the fucker is barely bleeding. That's not good enough. It also proves to me that Dragon didn't try hard enough to find out the needed information. If Nicole was the one in danger the bastard would be missing body parts, or at the very least he wouldn't be able to look at me from two good eyes. To me that is just further proof I have to do this. Dragon is blinded by his need to keep things calm because of Nicole being pregnant.

"Alright fucker, time for round two."

"I told your buddies the last time, I don't know anything."

"Yeah, well, *I* don't believe you."

"Man, you can knock me around for another day, but it's the truth. I don't have anything else to tell you."

"We'll see, there is one thing that you don't understand."

"What's that?"

"The last time, I wasn't the one asking the questions."

"What difference does that make?"

"I'm not going to be as nice."

"Man, you don't have to do this! I'm telling you…"

"Yeah, you aren't telling me nothing yet fucker, but you will. You will."

I drag a chair over in front of him. I straddle it and lean over the back.

"Looks like my brother worked you over pretty good, too bad you didn't give him the right answers."

"Man, I don't know anything, I'm telling you! I told your friend that!"

"My friend?" For some reason that strikes me funny as hell. This guy really is not made for this line of work.

"Please man, you got to listen to me."

"I don't, actually," I say, reaching in my vest pocket for cigarettes. I slowly take one out of the pack putting the others on a small table. I'll need them eventually. "I don't have to listen to a fucking thing you have to say," I add, lighting my cigarette. I inhale the nicotine, watching the asshole in front of me. "I only have to listen if you say something I want to hear. The only thing in question is if you're going to tell me what I want to hear."

"And if I don't?"

"Did you know I don't smoke? Nasty habit really. Hate the damn things," I say exhaling the smoke, while watching the orange glow flicker.

"Man, I don't think…"

"Only reason I pack smokes around is sometimes they come in handy. Do you know what they are handy for?"

"Man…"

"They make good lie detectors," I say reaching the cigarette over and touching the burning ash on his stomach. To his credit he doesn't cry out. We'll see how quiet he is when I move the burns down to his shriveled up dick.

"Damn it…"

"We're going to play a game."

"A game?"

"You tell me what I want to hear and you won't have to see what it feels like to have cigarette burns on your balls."

"Fuck, man…"

"I really hope you tell me what I want to know. I don't want to touch your nasty ass junk."

"God, please listen to me…"

I put the cigarette back in my mouth and slide the knife out that I keep in my pocket. He watches as I pull out the blade. It's just a small pocketknife, but then that's all it needs to be. I put the cigarette in the ashtray on the table across from me, getting ready.

"Don't worry, I don't expect you to be impressed with the size of my blade."

Asshole looks at me like I'm insane. Hell, he should.

He has no idea how close I am to the edge.

"You're not from Kentucky, so maybe you don't know about them. Have you ever had Rocky Mountain Oysters?"

Again, that stupid look. Fucker.

"Never tasted them myself, but it's basically deep fried balls."

"Oh shit, man, seriously…"

"Doesn't matter what really, pig, sheep, goats, even sniveling ass-wipe balls probably work. I don't want to touch your shit, so I figure my knife can fix it so they don't move around while I fry them. Sounds like a good plan to me. What do you think?"

"Man, I'm telling you, I don't know anything!"

"Well, I mean, if you don't want to do it that way I can just cut the fuckers off, it's not like you're going to need them."

I take another hit off the cigarette, let the nicotine calm me, and take a deep breath. Time to get the party started. I'm giving up everything, might as well make it worth it.

Chapter 13

NICOLE

TWO DAYS. I'M supposed to be married in *two* days. I want that more than anything, but I want it with Dani here. I want it without this feeling of impending doom. I stare at the engagement ring on my finger; it seems to mock me. Dragon doesn't seem to be upset with me for keeping secrets. There's that at least.

Today was supposed to be the day that Dani was to meet with Michael. I keep looking over my shoulder. What will Michael do when he finds out Dani isn't showing? Does he already know she's not here? I should have told Dragon about the meeting. I don't even know why I didn't.

I'm at the flower shop giving approval to the bouquets and tying up last minute details. Dragon sent Bull along to watch over me. I'm glad he's here, he's probably one of the brother's I'm closest to, but since the accident, he has changed. I'm not sure how to help him, but I understand it. Totally.

"Going outside, Nic, I got to make a call. Don't leave the store till I come back," he grumbles and I strain to hear him. He doesn't talk loud these days; it pains him.

He's got a nasty scar along the side of his neck and I know it bothers him.

"Okay, Bull," I nod looking at the beautiful pink roses the florist has put together with baby's breath and wishing Dani could see them. I hear the bell sound as the store's door opens, signaling Bull's departure.

"These are beautiful, Trish. I love them," I say honestly and hope she doesn't detect the sadness in my voice.

I hear her gasp and look up. The man who delivered the note from Michael is standing beside her with a gun pointed to Trish's temple.

"Ms. Wentworth, I'll need you to follow me quietly through the back without making a scene."

"Like hell I will," I'm not going a damn place with him. If I do, it'd be like signing my death warrant.

"You will, or your friend here dies. It's your choice."

My eyes lock on Trish's. She's crying and the sobs shake through her body. The man has his gloved hand over her mouth to prevent her from screaming. I look over my shoulder, trying to spot Bull through the shop's main window. His back is turned to me as he talks on the phone. There's no way to get his attention and I'm not even sure what he could do if I did. I turn back to look at the man.

"She's innocent," I try to stress.

I listen to the sound of the hammer cocking on the gun. It seems extraordinarily loud.

"Stop! I'll go. Just don't hurt her!"

He takes the butt of the gun and slams it on top of Trish's head. Her eyes roll backwards and she slumps against her captor, unconscious. He reaches out and grabs my arm before I can run.

"Don't make a sound. I can still kill your friend and you before anyone can make it to you. You do have a child to worry about, do you not, Ms. Wentworth?"

I nod stiffly once, then allow him to pull me and my child into the back room. I hope Bull finds us missing quickly. It's not much, but that hope is all I've got right now.

WE'RE IN A limo. The creep (my name for him) and I are riding in the back and someone else is up front driving. I can't see because the screen is up. We've been riding for a while, but I have no idea for how long. I can't think past this giant lump of fear in my throat. Eventually we stop. I look around, it's an abandoned grade school that the county shut down a few years back. The weeds have grown around it, the windows have been shattered here and there and the brick is faded and there are cracks in some of them. I've passed it before, but until this moment I never realized how evil it looked.

When the vehicle stops, creepy guy grabs me by the arm roughly and pulls me out. I'm not the most graceful person right now, so I fall to the ground. I wince as gravel digs against my ass upon impact.

Shit, that's going to leave a mark.

"Get up."

Gee, not so cordial now.

I have to angle myself to the side to get up, but eventually do. He grabs my arm roughly again and pulls me along to the front entrance. If Dragon was here he'd feed this man his entrails. I decide that if the baby and I survive I'll tell him all about the guy, so he will.

He pushes me inside, ahead of him, and it takes every-thing I have not to fall again. I look up when I finally come to a stop, but immediately wish I didn't. Standing in front of me is the devil himself. Michael Kavanagh. Realistically, I knew it would be him, since it was his henchman and all that kidnapped me, but I just didn't want to see the asshole again.

"Hello, Nicole."

"Asshole."

His face tightens in irritation. I know it's not smart to upset him, but I can't keep from doing it, to be honest.

"I see you are the reason for the decline in Melinda's manners."

"That probably has more to do with the fact you're a butt munch," I say back to him and I really wish I could control my mouth sometimes, because I know that is going too far. I should be more cautious, because it's not just me now, it's the baby.

He slaps me hard with the back of his hand. I stumble backwards, holding the side of my face.

"I would watch my mouth, Ms. Wentworth."

I really want to say more, but I bite my tongue hard to keep from doing so. The coppery taste of blood enters my mouth.

"You do know that Dragon's man has already discov-ered I'm missing and they will be on your ass any minute."

"I do know they'll be here soon, but it won't matter.

By the time those imbeciles arrive, we will have already made our deal."

"I'm not entering into any kind of deal with you."

"Oh, but you are, Ms. Wentworth."

"No, I'm really not."

He motions over to creepy dude. The guy nods and walks towards a set of double doors. It looks like it used to be a gymnasium for the school. Michael puts his hand on my lower back to steer me towards the room. My skin crawls at the feel of his touch and I jerk away, giving him a scathing look. I walk in front of him though, because I know arguing will only get me or my child hurt. The fact that I'm pregnant won't bother Michael at all. I'm sure of that much.

As we enter the room it's dark and musty. A small amount of light is filtered inside by tiny rectangular windows that line the top of the large, main area. Most of them are taped up or covered somehow on the outside, so you can't really see anything inside. I blink my eyes, trying to focus. That's when I see a small movement in the corner. I freeze, afraid they are walking me into a trap. It's a stupid reaction really, because *come on*, what could I do if he was marching me to my death? Still, it's there. Michael pushes me from behind to walk farther and I stumble trying to resist. Once we make it about half-way through to the room, creepy dude breaks away. I see him walking to a small doorway. It's close to where I had seen the movement before. I lose sight of him after that and I look back over my shoulder at Michael. He looks so smug and condescending all at once. How can one man be so cold and bone-deep ugly?

"Dragon will find you. There's no place you can hide."

"Oh Nicole, how you do warm my heart being so naïve. I'm not going to need to hide from Mr. West at all."

"Yes you…"

"No. I. Won't." He says, pausing with each word and saying it in such a way the certainty of it chills me.

"I…"

"You're going to do exactly what I tell you and once you do…? That in and of itself will do away with Mr. West."

"It won't happen…" I hear the sound of switches being flipped and a second later light from overhead comes on. It's still dim. Only about one out of every four lights work, but still it shows the shaded, barren room pretty well. There's cracked concrete flooring underneath an old worn-out gym floor in a faded burnt orange coloring. It has cement block structured walls that have been painted a white color and you can tell there used to be cartoon figures here and there drawn on them. I think one was Bugs Bunny because you can see the outline of his gray ears.

I can't take in the room any farther though, because I hear a dull moan to my right. I turn back around to face the direction the sound is coming from, and that's when I see her.

Dani.

I gasp and pull, trying to get to her, but Michael clamps hard on my arm and refuses to let me go to her. I twist and turn, trying to get free. He adds his free hand and grabs hold of each of my arms and holds me against him. My stomach sours when I feel he has a hard erection rubbing against my ass. Somehow, I think it's because he's enjoying the situation and his power, more than having me in his arms.

I can't stop the tears that fall when I see her. She's curled up in a ball, her dark sweater is torn and her white pants are caked with dirt, and the majority of it is in the shape of a boot print. She's looking in my direction. Still, I know she can't see me because her eyes are puffy and swollen shut. Her mouth has been bleeding, her nose still is. There's an ugly purple-black bruise running down her jawline and under her eyes which have the same horrific color. Her beautiful dark hair is caked in mud and maybe, blood. She's far enough away it's hard to tell. One of her hands is lying awkward against her side, and the fingers on her other hand seem to be at weird angles. She's breathing hard, labored even, and shallow. The sad wheezing sound penetrates my ears and though it's quiet, it seems to be screaming at me now.

"You fucking son of a bitch! How could you? What kind of sick fucking freak would do this to a woman? You…"

That's when he stops my tirade by shoving me and slamming me into the cement-blocked wall. I turn to the side before the immediate impact and try to wrap my arms around my stomach. It causes my head to snap back against the blocks and pain shoots through my skull. I can feel the cement scratch against the skin on my hands. The force of impact sends pain to the side of my stomach and into my back where my kidney is.

Fear swamps me. Did it hurt the baby? I try to take deep breaths and hold myself completely still, hoping against hope that I'll be able to feel the baby move. I need that reassurance. I don't get it. I hold my stomach harder, rubbing my hand where the brunt of the impact was.

"Listen well, Ms. Wentworth. You will do as I say because if you don't, then you'll find my lovely wife here in pieces. I'll mail one to you a day for the rest of your life. That is if I let you live. Or maybe I should take from you what you helped take from me? After all, I have eyes on your fiancé even now. I could take *anyone* I want, at *any time* I want."

Dani moans. I can't tell if it's because of what Michael said or from pain. I think she is mostly unconscious.

"What do you want from me?" I ask, my eyes are glued to Dani. In my head there are visions of Dragon and his brothers, of my child. I do my best to fight down the panic inside of me, but I can't, not completely.

"I thought you would see to reason. I'll tell you what, Ms. Wentworth, because you're being so intelligent in your decisions, I shall only demand things that will be easy for you to do. First, you and Melinda will be coming back to New York with me."

My hand goes to my stomach, rubbing where the pain still lingers. I can feel movement and it helps me breathe easier. *I'm fucking scared.* I have no idea how to proceed. If I can just get through all of this till I can get back to Dragon, he can fix this. *He has to fix this.*

"I…Dragon will never allow that."

"Oh, but he will. You will make him believe that you don't want this life for your child. You will not go through with the wedding. Once Mr. West is convinced, he'll turn his back on you. It should be easy enough, I hear he has his own stable of women available. I can almost admire him for that. It *somewhat* makes up for him having no breeding or class.

I let the insults to Dragon roll off my back, if I don't it will get me killed. It's not easy and had I not been pregnant, it wouldn't have stopped me. I just keep repeating, *'there's more than me to worry about, there's more than me to worry about'*. As mantras go, it kind of sucks.

"If I don't do as you ask?"

"We've gone through this. Maybe I should show you that I mean business? Would you like a piece of Melinda early? Small though, I still have plans for her so marring her beauty is not an option just yet. A finger perhaps? Or toe? Though, I did love when she would wear those stilettos. Donald? Take off one of Mrs. Kavanagh's fingers. It doesn't matter which really, except for the ring finger. I want her to have my ring on her finger and this time *I* will decide when it comes off."

'Donald' (though creepy guy really fits him much better) kicks Dani hard in the stomach. She weakly cries out as her body curls from the pain. He bends over and roughly grabs her hand yanking it towards him. He takes out a wicked looking hunting knife and hits a button so it unfolds.

"Stop!"

He doesn't, so I turn to the pig behind me.

"Make him stop! Don't hurt her anymore! I'll do it!"

He raises his hand and I look quickly over to see Donald has stopped, though I can see that there is blood dripping from Dani's finger.

"I'll do it! Just please don't hurt her anymore."

"You fell into line so easily, Ms. Wentworth. Should I take you on your word, you think?"

"I said, I'll do it. You're not leaving me with much choice."

"Well, yes, this is true. Still, I think you capitulated a little too easy."

"Just stop!" I cry and the tears have been flowing steady from me since I got here, but now the panic is all the way into my soul. I can't see a way out of this and I know even if I give the madman what he wants, he'll eventually kill Dani, me, my baby and maybe even Dragon and the rest of the crew. I'm not naïve enough to even make myself believe that I am preventing anything by giving into him. No, I'm merely buying time.

"For now, I will take you at your word."

I try and breathe slower, before I pass out. I'm wringing my hands at this point to try and keep the shaking under control.

I'm going to start carrying a gun.

The thought rings in my head. If I had a gun I'd shoot the bastard between the eyes and this mess would be over with. This makes twice now that life has exploded and I was defenseless both times. *This shit has to end.*

"Rest assured, Ms. Wentworth, if you do not adhere to the bargain we have made, I will make sure you and everyone you care about regret it."

"I understand."

"Donald will return you back to town. I'll expect to hear that you've broken off your engagement. If I don't there will be repercussions."

"I can't just break it off without reason, Dragon will

be suspicious!"

"That is not my problem, Ms. Wentworth, it is yours. I just warn you, do not push me. You will *not like* how I push back. You helped Melinda leave me five years ago. You were not so concerned with the problems that brought into my life or the consequences of your actions then. I suggest you do not get distracted by them now."

I don't answer. It doesn't matter. Nothing matters at this point. I let Donald lead me back outside to the waiting limo. Michael doesn't follow and it makes me sick to leave Dani with him. Again, I have no choice.

IT'S LATE BY the time Donald drives me back into town. He keeps stopping other places and purposely delaying my return. I don't know why and I don't ask. In fact, I don't say two words on the way back. There's nothing to say, and besides, my mind is full. I'm trying to think of a way to get out of this mess. I'm wondering what would happen if I go to Dragon and confess everything. My first instinct is to do what I'm ordered to do, but keeping secrets from Dragon has already turned out bad. Plus, I know that even getting what he wants, Michael will enjoy hurting anyone I care about. So, Dragon has to know. It's time I start trying to rely on my man and give him what I expect from him—complete honesty and faith. He deserves that.

I'm feeling better with my decision. I'll get back and have Dragon and his men go search the school for Dani. There's nothing that Dragon and I can't handle together.

Chapter 14

DRAGON

"WHAT THE FUCK do you mean she's missing?"

"I told her not to leave the shop while I went outside to take a call from an Army buddy. I wasn't gone over five minutes Drag, I swear. I go back in and she's gone. I was watching the entrance the entire time."

I grab the first thing I can find, which happens to be the whiskey bottle I was about to have a drink out of. Just try and relax around this damned place. The bottle explodes against the wall and it does not do one damn thing to make me feel better.

"You were supposed to be watching her motherfucker, not the fucking *door*. If all I wanted was the fucking door watched I would have sent a son-of-a-bitching prospect! Of which your ass might be again by the end of the fucking day!"

"Drag, man, I'm telling you my eyes never left that..."

"But it did motherfucker, because you left my woman alone and the backdoor unguarded and I know this because her damned cell phone was found crushed by the door!"

Bull doesn't respond, but then there's nothing else for

him to say at this point. Fuck, when did my club become such a damned mess? Did we have it easy for so damned long that my men got soft? This was a juvenile, stupid-ass mistake and if my woman gets hurt because of it I will gut Bull, friend or no friend.

"Drag, Nicole just called in. Frog went to pick her up."

I don't know if the sigh of relief in the room was from me or Bull. I just know those are the best words I've ever heard.

"Call the rest of the men off the search."

"Already done," Freak says heading back towards my office where he's been working, going over the tapes of the flower shop. The man who has been sneaking around my club is the one who took Nicole—a Donald Tover. He has ties to Michael Kavanagh and that in and of itself signed his death warrant. I will end him. I just have to plot how I'm going to do it. A man with that much power and money can't disappear easily. Worse, he'll be harder to trap.

"You, get out of my sight for now, go find Crusher and drag his ass back here!" I order Bull. It's harsh, but *motherfucker*, it feels like I can trust my prospects more than the original patched in members!

He gives me a look of disgust and leaves the room. It's another twenty minute wait and three shots of whiskey to calm my nerves before my woman walks through the front door. I'm practically on her before she takes one step in.

Before she can even speak, I have her wrapped in my arms. I inhale her scent, breathing deeper so I can take it all the way in.

"God, Mama," I whisper shakily into her ear, as I feel her arms go around me and hold onto me tightly.

Her nails are digging into my back with a fierceness that tells me just how scared my woman has been. I need to find out information, I need to hunt down the bastard responsible for it all, but all I can think right now is that I need Nicole. I need her taste, her comfort. I need the feel of her in my arms. It's a need so huge that I almost take her right where we're standing. I can't. I have to capture this SOB before he has a chance to escape. So for now, I push my tongue into her mouth and content myself with a kiss. It's a fucking great kiss though, full of heat and need. Our tongues fighting each other for control and my dick pounding with the need to be buried deep inside of her.

We break away slowly. She takes a shaky breath and rests her forehead on my chest. Her hands are gripping my biceps and her nails are still digging into me. It soothes me.

"Dragon," she whispers.

My name on her lips. Her taste on my tongue. That is all I need in life.

"Mama, talk to me."

"They have Dani, Dragon. He's demanding I...he's torturing me with her. He has Dani, Dragon."

I listen to her mumbled words and the fear in her voice physically hurts me.

"Where Nicole?"

"The old abandoned Laurel Elementary School. Dragon, we have to save her. She's in such bad shape."

"What kind of fucking shape?" Crusher picks that minute to come in the door and the anger in him at hearing Dani is hurt vibrates through the room. My brother has it bad.

"He…they beat her. She, oh God, I've never seen someone hurt that bad before. He'll kill her if we don't get her."

"We won't give him the chance. I got one of his men being followed even now, Mama. I'll find out where he's staying. In the meantime, we'll go check the school out."

"Okay, I'm ready to…"

"No, Mama, you're staying here. We'll talk about what you went through when I get back. Bull will watch over you and this time he won't let you out of his sight." I add that last part with a death-glare at Bull. He nods in agreement.

"But I need to be there for her, Dragon…"

"You need to think of our little one, Mama. I'll go and if Dani is there, sweetheart, I'll be careful with her and bring her back to you."

"I…okay, can Poncho check me out?"

"Shit, Mama, did they hurt you?"

"He just slapped me and pushed me. But he pushed me into a wall and I hit my stomach…"

"I'll get him right to you. I'll let Crush and the boys go to the school," I respond picking her up in my arms, intent on lying her on the bed and holding her until Poncho gets here.

"No, you need to be there to help Dani, Dragon. Please? I'll be fine, I promise. Little Dragon is already moving around. I just want to be safe."

I don't respond till I have her back in our room and place her on the bed. She looks so tired and beaten right now, but there's never been a more beautiful woman in the world.

"Are you sure?" I ask still not convinced and hurting at the thought of leaving her.

She takes my hand and guides it to the top of her stomach. It doesn't take but a minute, and I feel the strong fluttering beneath. Will I ever get used to that miracle? I don't think so. I bend down and place a kiss there. I raise back up and look at my woman—my life.

"I love you, Mama."

"Forever, Dragon," she whispers back.

I want to kiss her again but I don't. I'm so raw, that if I give in, I won't be finished with just a kiss.

"I'll be back," I say giving her one last glance and taking in her weak smile before I leave the room and close her door softly behind me.

"Bull, you call Poncho to get here and you do *not* leave my woman unguarded for a minute!"

"Got it, Drag."

I nod and turn to the door. "Load up, we're headed to the old school building on Old 25."

Crush is already gone. Just one more fucking problem at this point.

"Frog, you can take the SUV with me, just in case Dani is still there. The others can take their bikes."

"No need for sneaking in?" That comes from Hawk.

"Nah man, I don't look for them to still be there. I'm just hoping for a clue to where he might have taken Dani." I don't add that they wouldn't have left Nicole still breathing if she could lead us to them. I don't even want to think of that shit.

Kavanagh likes to orchestrate things, he wants a big impact. In this instance, that works to my advantage. I just need to make sure all my bases are covered before I retaliate, but I will. I'll come down on him like a blazing fire and when I'm done, the son of a bitch will not be breathing.

"Frog, who do you got tailing our man?" I ask getting in the driver's side of the vehicle.

Frog turns around and looks at me confused.

"What man?"

"The scumbag we've been holding to lead us back to Kavanagh," I say with a weary sigh, peeling out of the parking lot.

Frog rakes the side of his face.

"Uh, Boss?"

"Yeah?"

"Crusher came by the cabin and said you told him to deal with it."

"Say, what?"

"Honest man, he showed up at the cabin, said you told him he was in charge of letting the worm go and following him back to his Boss."

I reach down into my pocket and pull out my phone.

"Hello?"

"Yo, Dance, meet me out at the old elementary school."

"Sure, what's up?"

"A fucking lot. Need you there man, I'll explain then."

"You got it, let me just get Nailer here to watch over my woman."

"Have him take her back to the club, she can keep

Nicole company. We may be awhile."

"Got it. Later Drag," he says hanging up.

"Boss, I didn't mean to…"

"It's not you, man. Though from now own you double check all of my orders through me. You get me?"

"Yeah, I got it."

We're silent the rest of the way to the school. My club is a mess and the two men I thought I could depend on the most are the very ones fucking up.

"SON OF A bitch!" Crusher screams for the tenth time.

Just as I figured, Kavanagh and his henchman are long gone when we get here. The place is completely deserted, with one exception. There is a fuck of a lot of blood in the old gym. If Dani is still alive, she's in pretty bad fucking shape. Which explains why Crusher is going off. Yet, I'm so upset with the bastard that I'm about ready to snap his neck. I'm trying to rein it in. I'd rather deal with this shit in private.

"I knew you fucking around would end up screwing us in the ass. Now we have no idea where the hell Dani is!"

And this is where my restraint with Crusher ends.

My fist slams his punk ass under the chin with all my anger and since I have a lot of fucking anger, Crusher immediately stumbles back and falls on his ass. He's shaking his head back and forth, obviously dazed. He's lucky that's all he is. I still might pinch his neck before this is done.

"Motherfucker! That is not what screwed us in the

ass!" I growl squatting down so I am eye level with the bastard. "What screwed us in the ass, dick-weed, was you overruling my fucking orders. Tell me, where the fuck is my prisoner today, Crush? What the fuck did you do with him?"

Crush looks up at me, rubbing his chin and jaw. His eyes are bloodshot, his hair hasn't been brushed, his clothes are wrinkled, and his knuckles are scraped and bruised. Brother is messed up.

I grab him by the hair on his head and pull him to me.

"Where the fuck is my prisoner, Crush?"

"I did what you wouldn't." He says trying to jerk away from me, but I'm not about to let that shit happen.

"Yeah, and what was that, brother?" I growl, trying to tap down the anger so I don't kill him.

"I interrogated the ass-wipe."

"Gee, wonder why I didn't think of that," I respond sarcastically. "Tell me Crush, did you find out one more damn piece of information?"

His eyes lock with mine and then he shakes his head no.

I push him away from me in disgust.

"Do you know why that is dick-head? It's because he didn't fucking know anything!" I growl. "Did you set him free, at least, and have someone follow him?"

Crush avoids my eyes for a minute and then turns his head so his eyes, once again, lock with mine.

"There wasn't anything to set free."

I close my eyes and pinch the bridge of my nose, where I feel the tension starting to build.

Fuck, it's going to be a *long* day.

Chapter 15

NICOLE

I MUST HAVE dozed off. I have no idea when or for how long, but I do know it is dark now. Dragon is beside me, his front is to my back, spooning me. His arm is loose over our child, cupping my stomach.

"Dani?" I whisper already knowing the answer, but hoping against hope I am wrong.

"She was already gone, Mama," he says softly, the words seeming to haunt the room.

I can't stop the sob of pain that escapes my lips. I feel his breath against my hair and he kisses my ear, gathering me closer.

"We'll find her, Nicole. I promise you, baby, we'll find her."

I want to believe his words, honest, but I can't seem to. All I feel is that Dani is in trouble and neither one of us may survive this, because I have to help her.

"I'm scared, Dragon."

"I know baby. I know."

He turns me to my back and his large hand brushes along the side of my face.

"I'll make this right. I promise. I will make this right *for you*, Mama."

He's breaking my heart. He's blaming himself and he shouldn't. It was my secret, it was my lies that brought us to this point. I touch his lips with my fingers. My man. How empty my life was without him.

"I love you so much, Dragon."

"I feel the same Mama, right down to the…"

"Marrow of my bones…" I say with him, a weak smile on my face.

"We'll get through this. There's nothing we can't handle when we work together."

I wish I could believe that. I can't. I feel defeated.

"Do you trust me, Nicole?"

"You know I do."

"Then believe in this," he says and his eyes bore into mine.

I lean up and let my tongue dance over his nipple, he groans. I suck it into my mouth, while letting my fingernails drag along his side.

"What are you doing, Mama?" He asks his eyes closed.

"I must not be doing it right if you have to ask me," I whisper against his skin.

"Mama, you're upset and tired. You've had a rough day," he protests but even I can tell his heart isn't in it. Which is good, totally good.

I stop and look up at him so he can see the truth in my eyes.

"Dragon, I need you tonight. Poncho said I was fine. I just need to feel you holding me in your arms, so I can forget about everything but *us*. Give that to me, please?"

He pulls away from me and for a moment all I can feel

is disappointment. *Total disappointment.*

Then he pulls the covers from me. Up until this point his eyes have never left mine. Now they do. Now, they travel the length of my body and I feel the heat of embarrassment flush my face.

I've always had image problems because I wasn't skinny. Dragon has slowly made me appreciate my curves, but since I got pregnant I cringe at how my hips have grown, my stomach is so big these days I feel like I waddle, and I still have three more months to go. There is nothing sexy about my body, nothing at all. Every time I see a Twinkie get close to Dragon, I want to go running like a banshee, screaming and clawing her eyes out. Luckily, he never gives another woman the time of day. I think if he did, part of my soul would wither.

"Stop it, Mama," his gruff command sends chills through me.

"Stop what?"

"You are beautiful. Fuck, woman, you take my breath away every day. You have since the beginning," he says, sliding off the bed at an angle so he's stretched along the side of my legs. He runs his hands up my calves and the warm feel of him creates a friction that instantly makes me hungry for more.

I arc my head back as I feel his tongue slide along the inside of my kneecap. Who knew that was an erogenous zone? I think maybe with Dragon, my entire body is in that zone. He kisses along the outside of my thigh now, at the same time his hand is brushing on the inside. I know he can feel the wetness and the heat he has created. In that, I feel no embarrassment. He *owns* my body.

When his fingertips brush against my center, teasing the fine hairs that rest there, I can't stop a whimper from escaping.

"Nicole."

I hadn't realized my eyes closed until I hear my name. Slowly, I open them to find him looking down and smiling at me.

"I've wanted you and no one else, from the first moment I set eyes on you. The fact that you're carrying my child only strengthens that, Mama."

"You just wanted to get laid, Dragon. You even scoped out Dani," I argue thinking back to that day at the gas station, where I met him.

His eyes darken, somehow, and his face becomes harder. I know that look and I might be in trouble. Dragon's hands pull my legs farther apart. One hand moves to my pussy and instantly starts teasing my clit. No slow build up here, just an immediate punch of adrenaline and need. He must have decided I was wet enough to accept him, because without another thought, he lifts himself over me and thrusts inside, all in one fluid motion.

"How many women have I sunk my cock into since we met, Nicole?"

I bring my legs up so they cradle him on each side, and just that simple adjustment takes him deeper inside. Not as deep as I want, because Dragon is bracing himself above me, but still deep enough that the fact he is not moving, drives me crazy.

"Dragon, move, baby," I urge.

"How many women have got my dick since you came into my life, Nicole?"

I try to move for him, but without his help it just won't get us there. I groan out in frustration.

"Will you move?"

"Answer the fucking question, woman."

"None!"

"And how many woman have I looked at since that night at the Wolf's Den when I finally had you."

"Finally? Dragon, you fucked me pretty soon after we met. I was kind of a horn dog around you."

"Bullshit. You were magnificent. But it was *not* soon, Mama. Each day was a fucking waste," he argues, holding himself over me with one arm, while tangling his free hand in my hair.

"Dragon…"

"I'm only half alive without you Mama, it was true then and that hasn't changed. Hell, if anything, it's just stronger. You're my soul, woman, *my* very fucking soul."

Finally, he starts to move, his body an instrument that plays mine completely. His thrusts are measured, slow and methodical. When he moves his free hand down to torture my clit in unison with them, I can't hold back.

I disintegrate into a million pieces. Screaming out his name so loud I figure they can hear us three states over. It doesn't matter, nothing matters except Dragon. I want to wrap my legs around him and pull him tighter. I want to feel his weight rest on me. I can't have that, so I do the only thing I'm able to do at this moment.

"I love you. No matter what, I'll always love you, Dragon."

That seems to satisfy him because, with a moan of pleasure, he starts going over the edge and I watch. I watch every feeling, every drop of emotion, every small piece of happiness and pleasure that reflects on his face, I watch and commit it all to memory. I'm going to need it, because I'm scared Michael is going to win.

Chapter 16

DRAGON

TODAY IS THE day. My wedding. Never fucking thought I'd want it, and now I can't wait for it. Today is the day I make Nicole legally *mine*. It's stupid. In my world, papers and legal titles don't mean shit. You fight and earn what you get, you fight to keep it. Still, with Nicole, I want to have her in every way physically and humanly possible. That includes, my ring on her finger, and giving her my name. I want...no I need that. I always hated my name; found it just another thing the world mocked me with. Nicole made it okay to pass my name on to our son or daughter. So, this wedding is pretty damned important for a lot of reasons.

So important, I find myself wearing a damn monkey suit to make my woman happy. Fuck, I hate this shit. Still, my woman wanted one day filled with the dreams of her wedding that she has secretly harbored for years. Wearing a monkey suit to give her that dream? It seems a small enough thing to do. She's so upset over her girl and so withdrawn since she found out that Kavanagh has Dani, I'd do anything to make her smile even tying this mother-fucking-god-damned tie around my neck. Except I've tried a hundred times and still don't have it.

"Fuck!" I yell out, looking in the mirror of the small chapel and trying to tie the damned thing and failing yet again.

"Having trouble there, Drag?" Dance asks, walking in wearing his own version of the monkey suit, dress pants, white silk shirt, but buttoned down and no tie. My men may kill me. I'm not sure I'd blame them.

"Fucking-son-of-a-bitching thing, I can't get it tied."

Dance comes over and starts to work on my tie, the smart ass look on his face pisses me off, but I've got enough fires going. I'll beat him down a different day.

"Any word from Crush?"

"No, not since he stomped out of the school the other day."

"He'll come around, Bro'."

"I'm not so sure, but that shit needed to be addressed."

"What about Bull?" Dance asks backing away from me as I look in the mirror. The tie is fixed perfectly.

"Who taught you how to do that shit?"

"I'm a man of many skills, Drag-o."

"Whatever," I say adjusting the tie.

I'm tempted to yank that shit off, but I don't. I'm already feeling guilty because I know I'm pushing Nicole into the wedding today. She would rather call it off and wait until we get Dani back and Kavanagh is not an issue. She told me what Kavanagh said he would do. I'm convinced going against him is the only way to draw him out. I need for him to lose control. Men who are not in control get sloppy—they make mistakes.

Plus, I want this marriage done. I do not want to wait. Hell, we've had too much of that shit and things keep coming our way. If I don't get my ring on her finger soon, we may never get married and that is *unacceptable*.

"So, really, have you talked to Bull?" Dance asks again.

"No, something going on?"

"You see how he is. Brother's got shit muddling in his brain Drag, I see it miles off and I think he's pissed at the ass chewing you gave him over Nicole."

"She could have been killed, Dance. He knew better than to leave her alone."

Dancer holds up his hand.

"I hear you, brother. I'm just saying, you're doing an awful lot of ordering Bull around to do shit, that normally, a club enforcer does not do. And shit he used to do, you're not relying on him to do. Brother has a crap load of shit to work through, but not having the trust of his Prez, well it ain't going to help, Drag. That's all I'm saying."

"Moving in with a woman and living out of the club has turned you into a weeping whiney vagina," I grumble turning my back on him. He actually has a point. I haven't been calling on Bull to handle shit. He needs time to recover and he has issues with strength right now. I should have talked it over with him though. If I can just get through this damn wedding, I will.

"Fuck you, I'm not the one wearing a tie and standing before a preacher."

"You would if Carrie demanded it."

"Care Bear wouldn't. That's why she's perfect for me."

"Whatever. She's got a bun in the oven, women go bat-shit crazy when those hormones start talking."

"Odd, from where I'm standing it's you that seems all gung-ho for the wedding, not the bride."

I flip him off. He's right and I don't want to fucking talk about it.

Bull and Freak pick that minute to walk in. They're dressed like Dance. Hell maybe I should take the tie off too, just so we can match? Women like that shit right?

"Drag, we got some problems."

"What do you mean problems?" *Fuck*, I knew something was going to happen, I just knew it.

"Torch was going through surveillance video and found Kavanagh's man visiting the church this morning," Freak says and I want to rip his face off.

"How the fuck was this not caught the minute he stepped foot on the fucking property?"

"Don't look at me, it's not like you put me in charge of security, Dragon," Bull says and shit, he's right, plus this just adds strength to Dancer's remarks earlier.

"Do we know what that son of a bitch did while he was here?"

"Cameras lost sight of him for about five minutes so he couldn't have done much," Freak says, but he's wrong.

"You can plant a motherfucking bomb in five minutes. Do we at least know in what direction he went?"

"Toward the rooms the women are using," Freak says raking his fingers through his beard.

I look at Bull. "You're in charge, get this place on lockdown and find out what the son of a bitch did!"

Bull looks at me funny but he doesn't say anything. He nods once and takes off behind Freak. I follow them out the door with Dancer on my heels. I need to make sure

Nicole is okay. Then I need to kill some people, because I'm pretty sure right now that's all that will make me feel better.

Chapter 17

NICOLE

MY WEDDING DAY. It should be a day filled with joy, excitement and dreams being fulfilled. Instead, it's raining and the dark clouds outside seem like a beacon for evil. Evil that's threatening me at every turn. I keep looking over my shoulder, expecting to see Michael or his goon Donald. I'm anticipating the sound of gunfire and having dead bodies littering the church pews. *These* are *not* the visions a bride should have the day of her wedding.

I look in the mirror at my princess dress, fixing my hair one last time in the style that Dani and I had decided on. *Dani.* I don't want to get married worried and scared about what is happening to her. I want her with me. Dragon told me to trust him. He told me to put this on his shoulders and just go through with the wedding. He's convinced that we can do anything together, I love him and don't want to disappoint him. So I'm standing here at Faith Baptist Church, looking in a mirror at my perfect dress and preparing to walk down the aisle to the man I love. My hands are shaking at the thought. Not because of bridal nerves, no, that would be too *normal*...I'm going against direct orders from Michael. What will he do to retaliate? It's a situation no woman should have to face. How can I get married to Dragon with everything going on with Dani? Can I disappoint Dragon, knowing I love him with everything inside of me and he's convinced this is the right thing to do?

Before I can get lost in more dismal thoughts, there's a quiet knock at the door. I turn around just as it opens, and Carrie is standing there in her pink bridesmaid dress, holding her bouquet of white roses. The opposite of mine, since I have pink roses for my bouquet. She really is beautiful. Dani and I decided to go sleek and sexy with the bridesmaid dresses and I really love them. She's also holding a small blue box with a matching ribbon on it.

"You look gorgeous!" She says and it makes me smile.

"I was just about to say the same about you. Dancer will flip when he sees you."

"I'm just about to go show him. This was delivered to our room instead of yours and it has your name on it. It's a Tiffany box, so I thought it might be something you want before your wedding."

"Really? I wasn't expecting anything."

"I bet Dragon wanted to surprise you," she says handing the box to me. There's no tag on it, other than the signature Tiffany blue box and ribbon.

"Damn! Care Bear, how am I supposed to let you walk down the aisle looking like that?"

I look up to see Dancer and Dragon come to the door. My eyes lock with Dragon's. I see the worry etched in his face and I hate that I put it there. I can't change it though, and the fact that he has now seen me before the ceremony on our wedding day just jumps out at me. *Like we need any more bad luck.*

"Dragon! You're not supposed to see me!"

"Bullshit, you're mine. I want to see you, then I see you."

Damn man is so irritatingly cocky. It's a good thing I love him.

"It's bad enough we slept together last night, God knows we don't need any more bad luck."

"Woman, you are not spending a night out of my bed. It's not happening. Same with the other shit. We're not going to listen to old wives' tales."

I just shake my head. I could talk until I'm blue in the face and it wouldn't do any good.

"Care Bear, I got something I want to talk to you about. Come outside with me for a bit by the church gazebo."

"Something you want to talk to me about?" Carrie asks and I laugh as I watch Dancer move his eyebrows back and forth.

"Let's go outside and we'll talk about the first thing that pops up."

Carrie seems confused for a minute and then slaps him playfully on the arm.

"You're like a giant kid," she says but I notice she lets him lead her from the room.

They laugh and joke as they leave and I smile. I'm glad they finally seem to be happy. I look up at Dragon and the smile freezes on my face. He's tense and worried. I've seen that look too many times to mistake it now.

"What's up?"

"Nothing, baby, I was just checking on you, I needed

to see you."

He's lying. I know it. I decide to let him get away with it.

"No word on the men you have searching for Dani?"

He shakes his head and even though I knew the answer before I asked, the response still hurts.

"Come outside with me for a little bit. The men want to check the rooms and everything to make sure it's safe."

My world stops.

"Why wouldn't it be safe?" I question, my voice coming out squeaky and fear is bleeding through the words.

"One of the cameras picked up Kavanagh's goon. I want to make sure he didn't leave us any surprises."

My heart picks up in speed at his answer. I grab my bouquet and the Tiffany box and let him lead me from the room.

"I told you we should have waited, Dragon. He told me not to go through with this."

"I told you, I'll handle him. I just have to find the son of a bitch first, and I will."

I want to argue. It won't do any good and to be honest, I'm just worn out. I think the term emotionally-drained applies well here.

"So much for a happy wedding. This is the wrong thing to do, Dragon." Okay so I'm a bitch and I can't help but voice my opinion for the hundredth time, just like I have for the last two days, even though he refuses to listen to me.

"Mama, damn it."

I just shake my head. I don't want to hear it. I don't want to fight with him on our wedding day either. I decide to concentrate on something else. I look down at the Tiffany box I'm holding in my hand.

"What did you get me? The delivery man had it delivered to the wrong room, Carrie just brought it to me."

"I didn't get you anything Mama, maybe it's from your…"

It takes me a minute to undo the lid because I'm holding my bouquet in one hand, but I finally get it. Dragon stops talking, or my scream drowns him out. It was one of those, because lying there in the blue Tiffany backdrop is a finger. A *finger*. Worse, I recognize the bright red nail polish. *It's Dani's finger.*

Dragon takes the box from my hand. He's talking but his words are just blurred out by the bile churning in my stomach and begging for release. I can't make his face out through my tears. I knew this would happen. I knew it. I tried to tell him but he wouldn't listen. He begged me to put my faith in him and I did and now look what I've done. *Oh God, what did I do?*

My bouquet drops to the ground, as people start making their way to us. I love Dragon. Right now, I long to wrap my arms around him, begging him to take me away. I can't. I did this, *we* did this. I just keep replaying Michael's words in my head. I should have listened. I didn't. Dragon's pleading with me but I can't ignore this. I don't have a choice. I want to run to him but I can't.

I run away.

Chapter 18

DRAGON

*M*OTHERFUCKER THAT'S THE word that enters my brain when Nicole starts screaming. I look down at the box and immediately know what that twisted fuck has done. It's been done so many fucking times it's cliché, but I guess that doesn't matter to a psychopath. Worse, the fact that it's a woman's finger. No, scratch that, it's Dani's finger. I'm not stupid. I take the box from Nicole and close it quick. I know that doesn't help, what has been seen can never be unseen.

Her beautiful blue eyes are looking at me so wounded. Tears are pouring down her face, but even through them, I can see the accusing glare. She asked me to postpone the wedding. She begged me, and I didn't listen. I should have. I thought I could control things. I need to fix this, but for the life of me I don't know how. Chances are Dani is dead. If she's not, she probably wishes she was. I still believe she'd be that way, even if Nicole and I had called the wedding off. I expected Kavanagh to go off the deep end. I just thought he would strike back at me instead of a woman.

I want to take Nicole in my arms, but I have the damn

box. So instead, I just stand there.

"Mama, stop. I'll get him. He's starting to lose control. That's what we need," I say but my words sound hollow to me.

"Lose control?" She screams. "He cut off her finger! He did exactly what he threatened! We shouldn't have gone through with this! I told you! I begged you to listen to me. This is *our* fault, Dragon. *Ours!*"

"No, Nicole. He would have done something like this either way, he likes being in control. We just have to make him get sloppy now."

"I'm done listening to you," she says and the pain in her voice alone could bring me to my knees.

I'm trying to explain. I can see it's not helping. I'm at a loss.

I can do nothing but watch her walk away. Watch as the woman I love leaves me standing by her bouquet. The bouquet it took her a fucking month to pick out is now thrown down like garbage. It lies there on the broken sidewalk mocking me. Nicole leaves me standing, without a backwards glance.

"Fuck, Boss, what's going on?" Freak asks, as Bull, Frog, Dancer, and Hawk come running.

I look at Bull. He's club enforcer I know, but he's also the one Nicole trusts the most, besides me and Crusher.

"I need you to go after Nicole, get the other women and take them all to the club. Get Six and the prospects and put the club on lockdown. Don't let her leave, Bull, she's going to want to. You can't let that happen."

"Boss…," Bull starts to argue. I just shake my head no.

"Please man, she's not thinking with her head right now." I've never said please to one of my brothers before. Fuck, other than it having to do with Nicole and sex, I don't think the word is in my vocabulary.

Bull must understand how desperate I am. He nods, slaps me on the shoulder. I toss him my keys to the Tahoe I drove this morning.

"Take Frog with you."

He nods and starts to turn away.

"Bull?"

"Yeah, Boss?"

"Keep her safe." He gives me a grim smile, takes the keys and tosses them to Frog.

"I got my truck. I'll pick Nic up. You get the other girls and get them to the club," Bull tells Frog and I agree. I need everyone safe and accounted for.

"I'll go help Hawk settle the crowd and have the girls meet me out front. We'll be there in thirty or forty minutes at the most," Frog says. Bull waves in acknowledgment and then takes off.

"I want Kavanagh found, and I want him found like yesterday. You feel me?" I tell the other men. They nod in agreement. "Freak, you're in charge, do whatever you have to do, call in any marker, make a deal with the fucking devil himself! I do not care, but I want the fucker under surveillance by nightfall. Hawk, go with Frog, shut the wedding down and make sure the women are back at the club, safe. Dance, you're with me." I turn away ignoring everyone else, still clutching the box in my hand.

"Drag, man, what the fuck happened?"

I shove the box at him.

"He sent Nicole a present! Dani's motherfucking finger! I want him found then I'm going to kill him!"

"Fuck…"

"Yeah."

"What are you thinking?"

"I got a plan. He thinks he has brought us down and has Nicole and Dani where he wants them. I'm going to let him think he's won."

"How are you going to do that?"

"I'll explain on the way back to the club. Any luck finding Crusher yet?"

"No, man. Freak has a few of the new prospects out searching for him in the usual haunts, he'll show soon."

"Let's hope so. I need him but only if his head is clear."

"Well, that box ain't going to help."

I don't argue. I know it won't.

"Where's your ride?" I ask. "You can drive while I fill you in on what I want to do to trap this fuck-wad."

"Parked beside yours, man."

I let him lead and glance over my shoulder, one last time, in the direction that Nicole disappeared to. I hope Bull can keep her from leaving the compound. I know she has it in her head to go to Kavanagh, and that can't happen.

We pile into the Tahoe. I watch through the windshield, as Freak, Hawk and Frog walk back towards the main chapel. The sight of the church hurts me. Fuck, Nicole may never talk to me again.

My phone rings and I look at the number on the display. *Shit.* I wonder what other fuck-ups happened today.

"Yeah motherfucker, want to tell me where you've been?"

"Drag, listen quick man."

Crush's voice comes over my phone, there are pops and crackling in the line and I can barely make him out.

"Where in fuck are you? Do you know what went down today?"

"Do…. Use… today…"

"What are you saying asshole, I can barely hear you?"

"Man… Car… Just now… got Dani but …"

"You got Dani? Fuck, man your signal sucks. Where'd you find her? We'll…"

"Listen can't…. you got to….use it today…get Freak to…"

The phone goes dead with me holding it in my hand.

What the fuck?

Dancer starts the vehicle up and Frog walks by with a slap on our hood. He climbs into my vehicle as I turn back to Dancer.

"What was that?"

"Crusher, I couldn't make out what he said, he said he had Dani… but he was trying to tell me something. Shit man, I couldn't make a…"

I don't get the chance to finish my sentence. The world erupts as pain hits me everywhere all at once and in all directions. An explosion blasts and heat rocks through the air.

Chapter 19

NICOLE

IT'S THAT MOMENT when you think life has reached rock bottom. That very second you feel part of you shrivel in despair. I've hit the bottom. There's no way I can feel worse.

I am wrong.

I leave Dragon behind. It hurts to look at him. I told him all along, but I can't let him shoulder the blame. I went through with it, knowing that Michael would retaliate if I went against him. I just didn't want to hurt Dragon. I wanted to be his wife. I was *selfish*. Is Dani still alive? Did the bastard kill her? I'm so engrossed in my thoughts, I'm not noticing anything around me. Which is a shame. I'm sure a bride with a stomach that looks like she swallowed three watermelons whole, hoofing it down the sidewalk of downtown London just as it starts to rain (which by the fucking way is just a cherry on top of a sundae) is a sight to see.

I scream when I feel a hand clamp around my shoulder. I expect to see Dragon. Part of me is disappointed when I don't. Which is crazy, since I walked away from him. Instead, there is Bull looking down at me.

"Need to get you back."

"I'm not getting married today, Bull," I argue, my voice is almost as hoarse as Bull's.

"I know. We still need to get you back to the compound where it's safe."

"I told Dragon we shouldn't have done this," I whisper looking down at the ground.

"A man can't bow down to others in this world, Nicole. You do and you're weak and you lose it all."

"So you do things that hurt people in your lives and say the hell with it because of pride?" The thought of Dragon being that way pains me.

Bull puts his hand under my chin, pulling my face back towards his.

"If men like Dragon don't stand strong, more than just Dani would suffer, Nicole. Drag carries a heavy load."

"She could be dead, Bull."

"Nothing Dragon could have done, would change that, Nicole. You two needed to come to him sooner. A man can only work with the hand he's dealt."

I look at him and I know what he is saying, but I don't have to like it. Still, I know he's saying the straight up truth. If I could go back, I would talk to Dragon the minute we first got Michael's note.

"Let's get in the truck. It might not be safe here."

I nod, following him like a lost lamb. Once we get settled, he starts the truck and turns on some music. We drive down the road in silence. Bull doesn't talk much and I can't function enough to talk. If I close my eyes I can still see Dani's finger. The bastard took the time to clean the finger and wipe any blood around it. He placed her pinky finger into the box, like a fucking trophy. Was she alert when he did it? Did she know? *God, is she breathing?*

A fire truck passes us with its sirens on and pulls me from my morbid thoughts.

A few minutes after that an ambulance and a rescue squad truck go by.

"Wonder what happened?" I question out loud.

Bull remains silent. When we pass two more emergency vehicles, I notice he is watching them in his side mirror. He still doesn't say anything. So I shrug it off. Maybe I'll hear what happened on the news tonight. If I even stick around. I figure Michael will contact me. Do I go to him? If I don't will he kill Dani? Has he already? If I do, he'll kill both of us. Unless…I manage to kill him first…

Bull's cell phone rings and distracts me before I can continue planning. I need a plan…

"Yeah?"

"Fuck! Who's hurt?"

"We'll be right there!" Bull yells into his phone and immediately starts cutting into the opposite lane to make a U-turn. He swerves yet again before our turn is complete. This time he cuts back in our original direction and lets out a stream of cuss words that would make a sailor blush. "Fuck! I need to be there! Yeah, okay but you better tell me the minute you know something you son of a bitch."

He growls, tossing his phone onto the empty part of the seat between us.

"Bull, what's wrong?"

"There was an explosion at the church…"

"Oh no! Bull, we have to go back!"

"I can't the cops aren't letting anyone in and I'm supposed to take you home and keep you safe until…"

"Screw that! You can turn around or I can jump out and walk back!" I argue.

Bull seems to have a war with himself, but in the end, decides to turn around. He flies, heading for the church. I know we're breaking new speed records getting there, but it seems like we're crawling. As we approach the church, I can see smoke and police cars blocking the road. Blue and red sirens are going crazy and there are uniformed cops standing in front of squad cars, blocking the main entrance. It's far enough away that I can't get a good look. I take off running, my arms cradling my stomach. These damn heels keep me from being able to get any speed, so I kick them off. I reach the cops and they try to hold me back, but by this time I can see Dragon's Tahoe and the one beside it—or what is left of them. They are charred and smoking and one of them is still burning. The flames are engulfing the seats on the inside. You can make out nothing, but the heat, even at this distance, is stifling. I scream trying to get through. I need to find Dragon… I need, oh God, I *need* to find Dragon.

I feel a new hand on my shoulder and the ones around my chest lose some of their rigidness. I could get away now, go to the cars. I could, but Bull's voice and the pain in it stops me.

"Nic girl," he says and his words are quiet, but they reach the haze I'm in, and I am in a *haze*. I don't even know half of what I'm feeling, I have no idea of anything around me. I am in *shock*. I look up at him, and the pain in his eyes pierce my heart. Standing beside him is Dancer, his face black, cuts scattered across his face. There are bandages seeped with blood on his hands, but it's his eyes that pull me in. Dancer has these brown eyes that have always caught my attention, but now there is something else in them. Something I don't want to see. So, I turn from them. Looking at Bull, praying for something different from him. I shake my head back and forth in denial of words not spoken aloud, but that are heavy in the smoke filled air.

"Nic, girl…," he repeats again. With just those two words, Bull pulls me in. His gruff, quiet voice sinks deep into my heart, and the dam breaks. The tears that were streaming down my face are nothing compared to the sobs that rock through me as I collapse against him.

"No!" I scream out in anguish. "No," I moan against his chest. The single word extending out as if it was the longest word in the English language. Bull tightens his hold and keeps me from falling to my knees. "Dragon…" I cry out again.

"I'm sorry, Nic. I'm so fucking sorry."

I don't know who said that. I don't even care. I'm too lost in misery.

I'm too…*lost*.

Chapter 20

CRUSHER

THERE IS A limit to what the human spirit and body can bear. I watched it accumulate for years with my mom. She was broken. She was dead inside way before her old man dealt the final death blow. So seeing Dani now curled in a corner, her face unrecognizable. Her body so beaten, so bruised and bloody that she looks as if she has been hit by a semi-truck—my heart stops.

I wasn't honest with Dragon. Maybe, I should have been. If I had told him how far I went to get the smallest glimmer of information from the rat he was planning on letting loose, what would he have done?

Would he have congratulated me, patted me on the back? Would he have told me I did a good job? Somehow I highly doubted it. So? I kept shit to myself, buried the body out in the forest away from hiking trails and set about finding Dani.

This Kavanagh's patsy we captured, did indeed know next to nothing. He let something slip though, as I was branding off anything that might be used for identification purposes. Whoever hired him, it wasn't Kavanagh himself. It was someone different and in one of their conversations the man had mentioned an old Tobacco Barn on Route 11. That small morsel of information allowed me to finally give him what he had been begging me for. Death. I thought about waiting to see if it panned out, but truly he didn't know anything else and I was running out of things to torture him with.

Part of my stomach twisted at the shit I did to him. Then I would shrug it off and picture Dani and what I knew was happening to her. I don't know how I knew she hadn't got away, *I just did*. Sometimes her face in my thoughts would be overshadowed by that of another—a woman from my past I couldn't help. So, I know I'm not acting rationally. I can't stop it, and most of me just doesn't give a fuck by this point.

I did take the time to bury the body, even though a huge part of me didn't want to. Then I hightailed it out to the old barn to see if there were any signs of life. Now, I'm standing outside of the barn peeking through a large crack. Dani, and to be honest I can only tell it is Dani by the mass of thick brunette hair, is curled in a half ball. She is so beaten, swollen and bruised it doesn't even look like it could be her. Her thick half-curly, brunette hair says it *is* though, even if it's caked in dirt and blood. Off from her are three men in suits standing and talking back and forth like they don't have a care in the world. I start to go in immediately and take them all out at once. It doesn't matter that there are three of them and only one of me. I have surprise on my side. I even start to do it, when I hear one of the men talking...

"I planted the bomb in Dragon's vehicle. It'll go off when he takes it out of park."

One man hits the guy who just spoke up on the back of the head.

"It didn't go off earlier today."

"Ow," he says grabbing his head. "It wasn't supposed to. I set the system up, it'll go off *now*, when the gearshift is moved from park. You said you wanted them both to pay, Boss."

Fuck. I need to get a call out to Dragon and warn him. I can't take the time to do it now though. Doing so, would risk being found and not being able to help Dani. I pray I get through before it's too late. It twists in my gut that I'm choosing Dani over my brothers, but it doesn't stop me.

"It better go off. You fuck this up and it will be the last thing you do. I'm leaving you here to watch over our prisoner, while Donald and I go see if we can catch the aftermath of it all. There better be *aftermath*, too."

"There will be, boss."

I push up against the barn as they go out the front entrance. I peek around the corner to see them get in a sleek black car that screams money. When they drive off, I take a breath of relief. While I'm waiting for them to be gone long enough so I know they won't try and circle back and catch me, I try and call Dragon.

It rings twice.

"Yeah motherfucker, want to tell me where you've been?"

"Drag, listen quick man." I say, knowing I don't have much time and honestly I don't want to hear it. He and I are going to have it out soon.

"Where in fuck are you? Do you know what went down today?"

Dragon's voice comes over my phone, but it's faint at best. The line is full of distortion and noise and I have to strain to hear it.

"Do not use the cages today…"

"What are you saying asshole, I can barely hear you?"

"Man, listen the cars are rigged to blow. I got Dani now, but you really…"

"You got Dani? Fuck, man your signal sucks. Where'd you find her? We'll…"

"Listen, Dragon! I can't talk. You got to hear me. The cars? Especially yours! Do not use it today. Don't use any of them, get Freak to…"

The call drops.

Fuck! If it wasn't for fear of discovery, I'd have thrown the damn thing across the field. I try to call Dragon back and it won't connect. I try again and get the fake busy signal and look at the screen of my phone to see, *'Call failed.'*

That's it I guess. I hope he got enough of the conversation. I can't think about it right now. I have to get Dani safe. It's been long enough now that if the other two were coming back they would have, right? Shit. I don't even know how long it's been. *Fuck it.*

I quietly make my way to the front entrance, draw my gun and take a breath. Then I kick the door open, shooting in the area I last saw the fucker. As my eyes light on him, my gun trains on him and only him. I shoot him three times, which is all I have left before the hammer clicks and nothing happens. Doesn't take long to empty the chamber. I should have brought a machine gun, those fuckers are more fun. It doesn't matter though because the bastard is dead. I watch as his body falls to the ground. I feel nothing but the wish that I could have got the other two.

I'm not completely over the fucking edge just yet. I take the time to reload my gun. Now is not the time to get caught with my pants down.

That done, I walk over to Dani. I get down on my knees and try to check her out. The sight of her *hurts*. It was bad from a distance, but it's even more monstrous up close. She has to be dead. No one could survive this kind of beating, especially a woman as small as Dani. I should have gotten here sooner. My hand trembles as I move it to her neck which is colored with…rope burns? *Did they strangle her?* I try to move her hair, but it's so caked with mud and… shit, it's soaked in her blood. I slide my fingers to her throat trying to find a pulse.

I find nothing.

"Oh fuck, Hell Cat, don't do this to me. You've got to survive, to punish this S.O.B."

I go down flat on my ass, feeling the hurt and pain seep into my system. I let another woman down; I was too late yet again. I reach out for her hand, needing to hold it… To take just a minute to tell her how sorry I am for letting her down. I pull her hand to me and yell out in denial as I see her fingers. Her beautiful hand, that I've felt slide over my body countless times in the last little bit is now almost as unrecognizable as her face. Her fingers have been broken and they're swollen and distorted, bending in ways I'm not sure can ever be straightened. Then I notice she has no small finger. It has been cut right at the base of the hand. The wound is open, angry, and so infected that if she were still breathing… *Motherfucker.*

I scream out in denial, as I pull her broken body over to my lap and I hold her hand in mine. She feels warm— not overly warm, but still she is not cold like death. I know because I have held death. I have seen death. I use my free hand to brush her face gently, because she's endured so much abuse you can barely make out the distinction of her features.

"I'll get him Hell Cat. I'll get him and make him pay, darlin'."

I kiss her forehead in goodbye and slide her off my lap when I hear it… It's faint, very faint, but I latch onto it immediately.

"Zander," her voice whispers, it is disjointed and full of pain.

"Oh fuck darlin', you *are* hanging on. That's my Hell Cat. I knew you had balls of steel. Let's get you home."

It takes me awhile, and I'm worried every fucking minute that we're about to be discovered. But, I manage to get her loaded into my truck. Every movement causes her pain. I find myself wishing she'll let herself sink back down into unconsciousness.

"Hang on a little longer, Hell Cat. Just a little longer and I'll have you at the hospital."

"No."

It was one syllable but the terror in her hoarse whispered voice spoke volumes.

"Hell Cat."

"Married. He'll…please, Zander."

Dani had never asked for anything. I didn't even know the word please was in her vocabulary. I should concentrate on that, but I find I can't. Instead I focus on the word that I do not like. The one word that makes me embrace anger. *Married.* My Hell Cat doesn't know it, but she's going to be a widow pretty fucking soon.

I call Doc and arrange to have him meet us at the club. Then I try constantly to call Dragon. Each time the call goes unanswered and I'm asked to leave a message, my gut clinches. Fuck. I hope I wasn't too late.

My foot pressers harder on the accelerator, but inside I feel like time has run out.

Chapter 21

NICOLE

I S IT POSSIBLE to function and be dead on the inside? I never really thought about it. Right now, I am thinking about it every minute. I'm forcing myself to go through the motions, but I just want to disappear.

It has been four days. Four long days since I've lost Dragon. I can't sleep, I don't eat and most days getting dressed is just too big of a chore. I haven't heard from Michael. I thought I would, especially after Crusher brought Dani home. Yet, there's not been a word.

Bull has locked the club down. No one is allowed out and very few get through the gates. The families of the men have all piled in and it should be my job to make sure everyone has a bed and the kids are entertained, but I haven't bothered. Hell, I guess technically it wouldn't be my job now. It would be whoever Bull designates. Crusher was the VP, but apparently he is not real high with the men of the club right now. He's also spending every waking minute with Dani.

Dani. Shit. She's in bad shape. I want to help her, but I can't even help myself. Carrie and the others have been working with her. They'll take care of her. I can't look at

Dani. Part of it is guilt, because I should have called off the wedding. A bigger part of it is anger because she brought Michael into my life and it cost me Dragon. I feel ashamed every time I think that, I know I cost Dragon his life. I should have told him from day one about Michael. I should have told him about Dani from the moment we started a relationship, but I didn't. I didn't call off the wedding, I didn't warn Dragon. I didn't do anything and I am the one who killed Dragon—even if I didn't plant the bomb.

Will Michael leave us alone now that he's had a small part of his revenge? I'd like to think so, but I don't. I know he is just sitting back, biding his time until he strikes again. I should be preparing for that. I'm not.

A light knock on my door brings me out of my thoughts. I don't make a move to respond or answer. Again, it's just too much damn effort.

"Nic sweetheart. We need to talk about the funeral," Carrie says and I curl tighter in the ball I've made of myself on the bed. I clutch my stomach. My child shouldn't hear the word funeral. Little Dragon shouldn't know he will be denied his father's touch, his father's love. It's wrong!

Oh God, please let me wake up from this nightmare.

"Nic…"

"Get out. Oh God, just get out!"

"Nic, we can't keep putting it off. I know you're hurting but…," she says walking to the foot of my bed. Seeing her doesn't help at all. What does she know about anything? She still has her man. Her child will still get to know her Dad.

"GET THE FUCK OUT OF MY ROOM!"

Carrie flinches like I hit her, I can't help it—I *do* want to hit her. I want to hit *everyone*. I want to *claw* them until I *draw blood*, I want to *scream* and *hit* them over and over until this hurt and rage inside of me disappears. I feel poisoned by it. My body feels tainted, dark and full of bitterness. So much bitterness I think I'm drowning.

"Nic..."

"Just go. Just go. Oh God. Just go..."

I keep repeating *just go*; I don't know how many times or for how long. I don't even realize that I'm crying. Can one person cry nonstop for days on end and not die?

"Leave us alone for a little bit, Red."

I hear Bull's voice, but I don't bother opening my eyes. I want to go to sleep and dream of Dragon.

A moment later I feel the bed dip with weight and then I feel arms pulling me up. Bull adjusts me so I'm leaning my head on his chest and he brushes his fingers through my hair. I want to pretend he is Dragon, but I can't. The *touch* is wrong, the *feelings* are wrong, the *scent* is wrong.

"You surprise me Little Mama, I thought you were made of stronger stuff."

"I miss him..."

"I know, I do too. We all do."

"It's not the same," I defend because they have no idea.

"I imagine it's not," he whispers and his voice breaks on the word not. I know it pains him to talk and really I think this is the longest conversation I've heard from him since the accident.

"I don't think I can do this, Bull. They want me to bury him. I can't."

He holds me a little closer, his finger still combing through my hair and he doesn't respond for a little bit. The room is quiet except for my crying. His heart is beating steady against my ear. Its beat is so strong and again, it reminds me of what has been taken away.

"You will do what you have to do."

"No…I just…"

It's then I feel him putting something over my arms. It's heavy and warm and it smells like… my man. God, Dragon's cut. The cut he always wore—except the one day I asked him not too. The one day that…

I cry harder. I can't stop the sobs that break loose. I don't know how long it goes on. I just know that Bull holds me through all of it and I'm glad. I don't want to be alone. Eventually I stop and just an odd shudder and hiccup comes through. I've soaked Bull's shirt. He doesn't complain.

"You have to pull yourself together Little Mama, if for no other reason than that baby you are carrying."

My hand rubs my stomach and I try to concentrate on his words.

"That baby needs a strong woman to see his way in this world. He needs someone to tell him about his Daddy and to teach him how to stand on his own two feet and become a man his Dad would have been proud of."

"It's not fair."

"It's life, Nic. It's just life. That's why you hold on to the good days a little harder. To make it through the bad ones."

"I don't think I held onto them enough."

"Do you remember them?"

"I'll never forget them."

"There you go. Make sure your boy has those memories to hold on too."

"You'll stay with me?" I ask suddenly panicked at the thought of being alone.

"As long as you need me to," he answers and I nod.

"I don't want a big fu...funeral. It should be quiet here at the compound maybe," I answer, choking on the word funeral.

"If that's what you want. We still will have a large convoy of bikers from all our chapters surrounding our brother to the cemetery. Then come back here for drinks and memories. We usually burn the cut to send up so our fallen has a safe journey, but I figure this should be kept for the baby."

I nod. "Can you set that up without me? I just...I can't, Bull. I'll try and be strong and make Dragon proud, but I just can't right now."

Bull kisses the top of my head and gets up, propping pillows under me.

"You got it, Little Mama. I'll organize everything. You just rest up."

I let him leave without responding. I'm just too tired.

Chapter 22

MICHAEL

I WATCH AS Donald falls to the ground. It didn't take much, two punches. Donald always was a weakling. He is however easily managed and it makes him useful.

"Mr. Kavanagh, I'm sorry. I do know how we can get Melinda back however."

I watch as he wipes the blood from his lip.

"Do tell me Donald, what brilliance has your mind come up with. I'm so intrigued. I'm sure it is something fantastic, since you can't even keep one prisoner in our grasp. A prisoner whom, I might add, could not even walk."

"The bastard's funeral. Word at the club they own is there will be a closed funeral, but the gates to the compound will be open to let all the riders out to follow the procession. They plan on riding their bikes to the cemetery. We could make our move then."

I listen to him and think about it. As plans go it is lacking, but the gates being open…with enough firepower I could take at least one of the bitches who owe me and demand the other in trade. Besides, I think playing with Miss Nicole for a while might be fun. She's got a lot more fire than I remembered. Women with fire are the best ones to break. I would have to cut that guttersnipe out of her first, still…that could be fun. The thought of having Nicole chained on my bed with her ass up in the air…just the image makes my dick jerk in reaction.

"We'll need more men. See if you can manage to get your ass up and do that much. When is this funeral?"

"In two days," Donald says, standing back up still dazed. I take satisfaction in that.

"Then get busy."

"Yes, sir," he states, stumbling his way out of my hotel room.

"And Donald?" I ask, just as he opens the door. By this time, I'm sitting on the sofa, staring at the television I don't have on. I don't watch television. I just prefer the view to that of the imbecile, Donald's, face.

"Yes, Mr. Kavanagh?"

"Do not fail me again. You won't get another chance. Do I make myself clear?"

"Ye..yes, sir."

"Very well."

The door clicks as he leaves. And I lay my head back, taking a sip of the scotch in my hand. This entire trip has been one failure after another. With the exception of Dragon West's death. That one turned out rather well. If only I had taken out the beautiful bitch Nicole with him. Still, this way I can make her suffer in other—more enjoyable ways. So, perhaps all is not lost. She's not exactly my taste, but she does have fire in her and I do so love to watch that crumble in a woman.

I look around the small hotel room. It's a two room

'suite', and using that word to describe it is laughable. This damn town has so little to offer. The air is starting to stagnate around me. This little safari into the Appalachian Mountains can't end soon enough for me. How people live like this is beyond me. I pick up the phone placed on the end table beside me.

"Front Desk." The grainy voice comes through after I dial zero.

"I need maid service, please."

"Yes, sir. I'll send them up right away."

"Thank you."

I hang up wondering what sort of specimen I will get today. Yesterday, she was nothing to look at. Still, I prefer watching a woman clean up after me more than anything else I could be doing. It takes around ten minutes and finally there's a knock at the door.

I walk slowly. I have nothing but time and I can't really travel freely around town. I'm sure the Savage MC knows by now who to blame for the untimely death of two of their own. Especially since one of them is their…oh wait, *was* their President.

I open the door to find a rather haggard, beat up brunette in wrinkled jeans and a faded yellow t-shirt. Not my taste on a normal day. She's slim, though, and if I ignore the wrinkles in her face and the sunk in haunted look around her eyes, I'll enjoy her.

"You called for a maid?" She asks and her voice is husky. Probably from a four-pack a day habit judging by the smell of her. I'll have to bathe her. There's no telling what I could catch from her otherwise.

"Yes, my bedroom and bath need cleaning. You may

start in the bathroom."

She takes off in the direction of the bath pulling along a cleaning cart. I tag the *Do Not Disturb* hanger on the door, close it and lock it. Why can't maids in hotels wear the black costume? It would be so much more appealing.

"What is your name?" I ask her following her into the bath area. She jumps. Oh look, I think I scared her. She has *no* idea how scared she should be.

"K...Kayla," she whispers turning to look at me. Upon first glance I would have imagined she was in her late thirties. Now I can see that she's just had a rough life. She's probably late twenties at the most.

"Kayla, tell me. Do you have a man at home?"

"I...I have a boyfriend." Her eyes are dark and probably her best feature. They go wide when she sees me push the cleaning cart back out into the main area. She looks afraid, which is good. She should be. Still, does she not notice the suit and the expensive diamond on my hand? She should consider herself lucky that I am lowering my standards this once.

"That is a shame."

"It is?" She slides to the side like she's going to get away from me. It's cute. They always run at first.

"Does he give you pleasure, Kayla?"

"I...I don't think we should be talking about this."

"I want to fuck you, Kayla."

She freezes and a blush enters her cheeks. Hmmm...that might be new. Even when I took Melinda's virginity she didn't blush. Perhaps I misjudged the pretty little Kayla.

"I...I can't. I'm in a relationship."

I take out my wallet. "I can afford to be generous. Plus, your boyfriend need never know.

"I…I don't know."

"Let's get the money out of the way? Shall we? A thousand dollars and you'll be on your way in an hour, maybe two."

"I…a thousand dollars?"

"Do we have a deal?"

"You'll wear protection?"

Oh please. Like I would ever sink into her unprotected. She scrubs toilets for god-sake.

"It will be a hardship, but I shall." I reach around her to turn the shower on. She jumps as my arm brushers hers.

"Okay," she whispers and the tear that falls from her eye makes my dick throb. Time to let the beast out to play.

I harshly place her so she has her back to me. I pull that hideous faded shirt off her and throw it to the floor. She gasps but unfortunately does nothing to fight me. She's wearing a plain white bra underneath. My first instinct is to destroy it. Instead, I unlatch and throw it to the ground. I grab a hand full of her hair, pulling her neck to my lips. I bite—not hard…not gentle. My nose curls in disgust, she smells like cleaning chemicals.

"I'm going to fuck you so hard, pretty Kayla, I will ruin you for any other man."

"Why…why me?"

"Take your pants and underwear off."

She hesitates for a minute and I pull her hair harder. "Give me what I want, any *way* I want it and you can take home five grand."

"Five grand?" She gasps, but I notice she is taking her clothes off more willingly.

When she is finally naked, I push her into the shower.

"Clean up. When you come out there will be clothes and perfume waiting for you. Do not keep me waiting."

She looks shocked. She has no idea the game she signed up to play. While she's in the shower, I lay out a red silk negligee that I often had Melinda wear for me. I also lay out her perfume. My dick is rock hard at the thought of punishing the bitch. Well, as close as I can come until I have Melinda in my hands again.

And...I *will* have her in my hands again. She *will* pay.

Chapter 23

NICOLE

THE CLUB HAS been transformed; it looks nothing like it normally does. I don't know who was in charge of cleaning and preparing for the service, but it does look beautiful. Still, I hate everything about it. I'm sitting in the front row, Bull on one side of me and Dancer on the other, with Carrie beside him. I can hear the tears being shed throughout the room.

I'm not crying. I have no tears left. I'm holding my man's cut in my arms. Our son kicks inside of me, he's been kicking nonstop since the service began. It's like he can feel the emptiness around me and is just as upset. Can he feel the difference in the air I'm taking in? How it is thin and insubstantial? How it does nothing to sustain me. Instead, the air burns my lungs. Each breath feels as if I am the one now dying.

I stare at the black granite urn on the pedestal in front of me. Frog's is a navy blue urn in an almost matching design and on a pedestal, too. I can't grieve Frog. I can't even try. My heart and mind is too consumed with Dragon. The service just broke. The members are talking, they're laughing or telling stories. Remembering Dragon and Frog in their own way and trying to hold onto them a little longer. I can't. I'm two steps away from falling completely apart. I can't do this; I can't let go of Dragon. I can't survive even a day without him, let alone say goodbye. He's been gone close to a week now. If it was going to get any easier, surely it would have in that time.

"Nic? How are you holding up?" Carrie asks. I feel bad that I've been less than nice to her. I think part of me resents her, because she has everything I thought I had— only she gets to keep it. I swallow down my resentment, it's not her fault.

"Considering I just had a service over an empty urn, and that I'm burying my husband...burying Dragon tomorrow? Peachy." Okay maybe I'm *not* burying my resentment quite so well. I can't even call him my husband and that just...*hurts.*

Carrie lets it slide, and my guilt increases. She doesn't deserve me being so shitty to her.

"I'm sorry," I whisper and she reaches out and holds my hand and applies pressure to it briefly before letting it go.

"Dani was wondering if you'd come by and see her."

No. My mind cries out. I'm not ready. I'm not sure I'll ever be ready. I close my eyes and I'm all set for my denial, when instead I nod my head in ascent.

Bull's heavy hand pats me on the shoulder. He's been at my side constantly. I don't think I would have made it through this without him. I look up at him and see approval in his eyes. I can't smile, but I give a faint nod and swallow down my fear of seeing Dani.

I follow Carrie down the long hall to Crusher's room.

He put Dani in there the moment he brought her back and he stands watch over her night and day. I've only seen him a couple of times, but the truth is, I don't think he's doing so great either. I haven't talked to him. I don't ask. I don't have the energy. He nods at us, as we walk past. His eyes have that faraway look in them I've noticed lately. I shrug it off.

Carrie knocks on the door, opens it and then stands back to let me in. I've barely stepped over the threshold before the door closes behind me. I know she shut it gently, but the sound of it closing seems to echo loudly in the room.

Dani's lying in bed. Her face is still swollen, and the bruises have taken on a purple and black shade. Her arm is in a cast, and her entire hand is splinted and bandaged up. I can't tell it from the cover that is pulled over her, but I know that her ribs are taped. Guilt swamps me, looking at her.

"Stop that Nic," she says and her voice is surprisingly strong, if not still hoarse. There are still rope burns around her neck where Michael had strangled her.

"Stop what?" I ask trying not to stare at her hand. Even if I can't see where the finger is missing, I know that it is not there.

"Stop feeling guilty, stop avoiding me, stop trying to keep it together in front of me. Pick one. Hell, pick all three."

"Well, you seem to have me all figured out."

"Sometimes, it's not that hard."

I let out a breath and sit down in a chair across from her. I'm wearing leggings and the red sweater dress that

Dragon always loved. I pulled my hair up high on my head so you can see the tattoo on my neck that declares I belong to Dragon. I do, I always will. I'm still holding his cut close to my stomach; I've not let go of it, really, since Bull gave it to me. Having it close, sleeping with it, makes me feel closer to Dragon. Last night, I even dreamed he laid down beside me. It was the sweetest dream I have ever had. I felt his arms go around me and my breath almost stopped. I told him I loved him and he whispered it back and asked me to be strong for our baby. The memory of that dream is the only thing that has kept me going today. It's the only thing that has kept the darkness from swallowing me whole.

"I'm sorry I can't be with you, Nic. I want to be."

"To be honest, I wouldn't know you were there. I barely know anyone is around."

Silence. It's awkward and stiff between us in a way that it never has been before. I don't know how to fix it. I don't even know if I want to try. I love Dani...I do. I'm just so tired.

"How's the baby?"

It bothers me that she doesn't call him Baby Dragon, since she has from the moment we found out I was pregnant. Dragon may be dead, but that doesn't change the facts that this baby is his.

"He's good."

"Zander says you haven't been eating."

"Zander...how did I not know that you and Crusher had gotten so close?"

"We hadn't—not really. It was just sex," she shrugs.

"What is it now?"

149

"I don't know. It's not sex now, that's for damned sure."

I nod, "Did Michael…did he…"

"I don't want to talk about it. Not right now."

I don't push, because I can understand that.

"I'm sorry, Nic. I know all of this is my fault and I'm sorry. I thought if I left, Michael would leave you all alone. I was wrong…and I'm so sorry. I know you probably hate me right now and I don't blame you. I'll leave as soon…"

"I don't hate you."

"Still, I've cost you so much and my brain is so screwed up that I just keep fucking up your life and I, hell I don't even know what I'm trying to say."

"I've made my own decisions, Dani. If anyone is to blame for Dragon's…if anyone is to blame it is me. I should have told him sooner about Michael. I should have trusted him and put him first."

Dani flinches. I scored a hit and I didn't even mean to, not really. I can't do this. Not now. Seeing Dani makes my guilt suffocate me.

"I need to go," I say standing up and walking towards the door. I *need* to escape.

"Nic, please. I'm so sorry…"

I turn to look at her and she looks so hurt and sad and it physically wounds me, but I can't give her what she wants. I *can't*.

"Being sorry doesn't change anything. Not a damn thing. I am sorry! I'm sorry I brought this into Dragon's world. I'm sorry that I put Dragon in danger. I'm sorry I let my loyalty to you overshadow my loyalty to Dragon. I'm sorry I can't go back. Because if I could, Dani? If I could go back? I'd choose Dragon! I wouldn't keep your secret. I would tell Dragon everything and not listen to anything you said. I would have slapped your damned face the very minute you told me I couldn't tell him. I would have…"

"That's fucking enough!"

I turn to look at Crusher staring down at me, his face flushed in anger and hate pouring out of his eyes. I embrace the hate. Finally someone is giving me what I deserve. *I killed Dragon.* They should all hate me instead of being nice to me. I'm so fucking tired of the nice.

"Oh look Dani your guard dog comes to your rescue. It's not enough, Crusher. It's not enough because Dani and I are to blame. It was our secrets that killed Frog. It was our secrets that killed Dragon! I destroyed the man I love. *I killed him!* And there's not a damn thing you can say that will change that fact. *I killed him!*"

"That's enough, Mamacita." I turn to see Skull standing at the opened door. Bull is behind him and he looks at me with so much sadness, that I have to avoid his eyes and look back at Skull.

"It's true."

"It's not. The only person responsible for any of this, querida, is the scum I will personally end. Now let us get you and the little one to your room. You should rest. Today has been stressful," he says guiding me towards the door.

I look over at Dani and she's crying, but I don't see hate in her eyes. I don't know why. I hate me. I allow Skull to lead me outside, his hand at my back.

"Dragon wouldn't like you being here."

Skull is silent for a minute and then says, "There comes a time in a man's life when things are out of his control. Alas, I only want to help you and the little one. So, it is okay si'?"

I don't reply. I don't think it would be okay, but that hardly matters now.

"You need to rest, querida. Tomorrow will be a very trying day for you," he says as we make it to the door of Drag…my room.

"I don't think that quite sums it up," I say opening the door.

"Yes well, some words have not been invented. Go rest. I shall be here in the morning to check on you."

I nod. I don't really know what to say to that. I don't think it would make Dragon very happy, but it's not even like that matters now.

I go through the motions of getting ready for bed. I pull on one of Dragon's shirts to sleep in. I even go so far as to splash a dash of his cologne on my fingers and rub it on my neck. I choose the very spot Dragon used to kiss after we made love. The aroma fills the air around me and I close my eyes and enjoy it. I crawl into bed hugging his cut close, losing time. I honestly don't know how long I lie there in the dark. Slowly, I feel my eyes grow heavy and I surrender to sleep. I feel Dragon all around me. His weight on our bed and his warmth at my back.

"You came back…" I whisper groggily.

"I'll never leave you, Mama. Never."

"But you did…"

"I'll always come back to you. Sleep, Mama. Stay strong for our baby."

"I love you, Dragon."

"I love you too Mama, forever…"

Even in my sleep the tears find me.

Chapter 24

NICOLE

I'M WEARING BLACK. I'm not a black person. Still, I'm doing it. I'm wearing a black silk slip dress, with flats because right now wearing heels is beyond my pregnant ass. I have on Dragon's cut over it and I feel horribly out of place. I don't even understand why. Maybe it's the clothes that just feel...wrong. It could be the fact that my stomach has grown so big you could serve a three course meal on it and I'm not even near my due date. It probably has more to do with sitting in this god-awful chair listening to the President of the Tennessee chapter talk about serving with Dragon overseas. He acts as if they were best friends. I can't remember Dragon talking about a Diesel. The fact that there was so much of his life that I didn't know irritates me. Why didn't I know? Why didn't Dragon and I talk more? We should have. We should have spent more time together.

There's a woman wearing a yellow dress that really is doing nothing for her figure. I don't remember seeing her before. She's not with any of the chapters. She's not wearing a cut that says she is property of one of the brothers. No one is really talking to her. She's in the next aisle across from me, about three rows back, but she's crying.

Dancer has been moved down the row today to make room for Skull. Why Skull feels it is okay for him to sit in chairs made for those closest to Dragon, I don't know. Dancer didn't argue; however, so I don't say anything. What could I say? Bull is still on the other side of me. I notice him giving Skull hateful looks, and had it not felt like my heart was being ripped out—I would have smiled. I elbow Bull and motion towards the strawberry blonde crying.

He looks at the girl. Leans down and whispers in my ear, "Frog's sister."

I grimace and swallow as a wave of sorrow settles, yet again. I've not allowed myself to think of Frog or the loss others might feel here; I've been consumed with my own loss. I didn't know Frog that well; I didn't even realize he had a sister. I should make an effort to say hi to her, but I figure I'm not going to. I should feel bad about that. I should feel bad about the fact that I'm going through the motions, marking time until everyone leaves and lets me disappear behind my bedroom door again. *I don't.* I just wish I could leave now.

"Are you alright, querida?" Skull asks putting his hand on my leg. I stare at his hand.

"I'd be fine if people would quit asking me that, and get your damned hand off my leg." I bark back and I don't do it quietly.

Diesel (whoever the hell he is) stops going on about how close he and Dragon were to look at me. Is it my imagination or is there a smile in those eyes. My back is killing me, I'm angry at the world and I feel like a sweaty elephant. I really might go off at any moment and that can't be good for anyone. I *should* be like Frog's sister. I'm not and I wonder if people are judging me because of it?

I'm cried out. There are no tears left inside of me right now and I'm *angry*. I'm mad at the club, the situation, this damned service, Dani, Michael, Crusher, Dancer…the list goes on. I'm so fucking mad at Dragon. I want to scream at him for leaving me. I can't. I can't do any of the things I feel the need to do. I am even more furious at myself. I *hate* myself right now and at the rate I'm going, probably will for the rest of my life.

Skull takes his hand away and Bull puts his arm around my back and squeezes my shoulder. I see a hint of a smile on his face and that should make me happy. It should, because Bull never smiles. Instead, I really wish I had a knife so I could jab it into Skull's hand when he absently pats my leg again. Hell, even a fork would work.

I shift in the seat again, as Diesel finally stops talking. He stops in front of me and holds out his hand for me to shake. I look up at him. He's tall, like really tall—close to seven foot. He's got a jagged scar along the side of his right eye. His hair is long and a dirty-gold-blonde, and he's got a scruffy beard, and tattoos on his fingers and arms that might be pretty nice-looking; I don't take the time to investigate them. I shake his hand. His grip is firm and swallows mine, completely.

"Very sorry for your loss, Mrs. West."

I didn't marry him! I want to scream. I didn't get to marry him. I didn't get to be Mrs. West and I should have! If I had married him, if I had insisted on continuing with the ceremony, Dragon wouldn't have got into the car. We would have gone back into the church and got married. Maybe Dragon would have gotten Crusher's call. The bomb would have never gone off and Dragon would be alive. Even if the bomb did explode, I would have been with him. *I would have been with him.* God, I want to be with him. The only time I feel like I'm alive right now is in bed at night when I dream of Dragon. When I can pretend he is still with me.

My baby kicks and guilt at my thoughts swamp me. I know I need to be here to bring our child into the world, but that doesn't change the fact that I don't *want* to be.

I nod at Diesel, words are beyond me at this point. Thankfully he leaves.

"What's wrong?" Bull whispers, picking up on my frustration. I don't know how to answer him. My body feels wrong? Being here feels wrong? I want to scream instead of cry? I want to draw blood? Without an answer, I just shrug.

Another member of the Savage MC crew stands up. This one is from the Georgia chapter; he apparently served with Frog. He starts talking about jumping out of planes and you can tell he really cared about Frog. I hear the sister's sobs get louder. I shift in my seat, again, as a sharp pain in my back stabs and then slowly disappears. Metal chairs are not comfortable on a pregnant woman, even with the pillow that Bull put at my back.

"Nic?" Bull asks and this time he seems worried.

"I'll be okay," I whisper, but I'm really not sure. The world seems to be going on around me and I'm just watching it. It's too late to be in shock over Dragon's death, right?

A little while later the service breaks. The crowd disburses out into the parking area; the men and their old ladies get on their rides. Bull and Dancer will be leading the crew. Crusher will be staying behind watching over Dani.

Does she know how lucky she is to have someone willing to give up the club for her? Because that's what he is doing, essentially. I've heard the talk. None of the men are happy with him; hell, I'm not happy with him. Couldn't he have left and made the call and then went back for Dani? He knew about the bombs. He *knew*. He could have saved Dragon.

Frog's family will be in one limo and I'll be in another, I'm not sure who with. I assume it will be Carrie, Nikki and Lips. I've not really talked to them since Dragon's....*death*. The word hits me. No, it throat punches me, because I can't catch my breath. Dragon's *death*. I'm sitting in the chair and my eyes go to the urn. The empty urn, because there was none of Dragon left. *Dragon's death*. Bull stands up at the same time Skull does. They both turn to help me out of the chair. I look up at them, but I can't get the breath to release from my chest to speak. I can't move. I feel the wetness gather in my eyes and I look back to the urn. *Dragon's death*. I shake my head back and forth in denial. Panic is setting in and I hate it. Anger is better, but I can't seem to grab it like I had before. *Dragon's death*. How will I go on without him? How will I raise our child without him?

Skull pulls me from the chair and guides me outside to the limo. I go, not by choice. I go because I can't breathe and maybe being outside will help. The harsh sun is bright and hurts my eyes. It seems wrong too. Everything about today is *wrong*.

"Ow…" I gasp as pain again hits my back.

"What is wrong, querida?" Skull asks and really his voice is annoying me.

Where did Bull go? I look around and see him climbing on his bike. *How special. Yet another member of the Savage MC choosing the club and their rides over me.*

"Pain in my back. Sitting too long, I guess." I answer licking my lips and looking around. The sound of bikes starting is all you can hear and the pipes are echoing in the air.

"Can you get into the car, or do you need to stand for a moment?" Skull asks. He's wearing a black suit and no cut. In fact if I didn't know him, I would not even know he is the President over his own MC club. He has an expensive air of a businessman about him. He always has.

"I…give me a minute. I need to catch my breath," I respond, and my voice is strained and distant over all the noise, but Skull seems to hear. I feel his hand at the base of my back and he's rubbing gently. I should complain, but I can't because it feels really good. Instead, I hold my stomach and try to breathe. The pain seems to be holding on longer than it had earlier. Maybe I have a kidney infection or something? I need to make an appointment for the doctor. I haven't exactly been taking care of myself the last week or so. The racket dies down as the bikes start pulling out. I look over my shoulder at Skull.

"I'm ready."

I'm not really, but I don't want to hold up the service

at the cemetery. Skull opens the door and I move to it, when another pain hits my back. This time it migrates into my lower stomach, and I nearly fall from the force of it. It *hurts*. I would almost think it was labor, but it's not in the right area. You don't have contractions in your back… right?

"Oh, shit." I groan as the pain intensifies for a minute before slowly letting back up.

"Querida?" Skull questions.

"I'm…"

"I wouldn't go any farther if I were you, Miss. Wentworth. Everyone keep their hands up please, so I can see them."

Just like that the day gets worse. I watch as Skull raises his hands. Then I turn to the voice that has haunted me for the last month. Michael is standing between two men. Each man has a gun pointed at me and Skull. I look at the other limo and there are three men with guns around it.

"What do you want? Haven't you taken enough from me?" I yell and I don't put my hands up, but Skull doesn't seem to worry about that. He is relaxed—almost cocky.

Michael smiles, but it's a smile which twists my insides. It's evil and cold.

"Not quite, but I will. Now we can play this two ways. You can come along quietly and your friends get to live. Or I can kill them all and still take you. The choice is yours really."

"What the fuck is wrong with you? All of this because you have a hard on for some woman who left you years ago? Man, do you have that much trouble holding on to a woman that you can't replace the bitch with someone else?"

My head jerks over to Six, who gets out of the front area of the limo. I agree with everything he is saying, but right now might *not* be the best time to say it. Michael looks over at Six, and I just know he's going to order the men to shoot. So, I try to distract him.

"You have to know Dani is in no shape to travel. It will kill her. Why are you here?"

Just as I predicted, Michael turns back to face me at the mention of Dani.

"*Melinda* will be coming with me. I thought only to preoccupy myself with you for now, but seeing as I've yet again managed to stay one step ahead of your dead boyfriend's club, I shall take both of you."

I ignore the way the words, *dead boyfriend,* hurt me. If I allow myself to think about it, it will decimate me.

"Querida, there's a gun at my back, in a holster. Lift up my shirt, slowly, and get it while Six is distracting him. Then you must duck inside for cover. Do you understand?" Skull whispers.

My heart is pounding in double time, but I hear. I reach down to feel for the weapon.

"What are you two talking about? You must know that there is nothing you can do." Michael says. I freeze afraid he will see me getting a weapon.

"Sure there is you sorry motherfucker, we can kill you." This comes from Torch who gets out of the limo; apparently he was driving. I thought when you rented limo's they came with drivers? The inane thought settles in my brain, as I take the gun and carefully slide it from the holster. I hold it in front of me, below my stomach so that it is hidden behind the car.

"Now!" Skull cries while pushing me down behind the car. I can hear bullets flying all around me. They're banging off the side of the limo and you can hear the pings as they hit like hail during a summer storm. Apparently, limos are bulletproof. *Good to know.* I slide inside the seat, figuring that was safer for the baby. Skull apparently had another gun because I can see it in his hand as he jumps in the car after me, sliding into the seat and pushing me along while he's at it. He slams the door shut.

"Shouldn't you be out there, you know, helping?"

"I'm doing what I am supposed to be doing. I'm guarding you."

"I'm in a bulletproof car, with a gun I might add! Just go out there and help Six, Nailer and the others!"

"I am thinking it is a good thing Dragon saw you first. Are you always tan mandona?"

"Could you, like, speak some freaking English and if you're not going to get out there to help them, I am."

"No, querida, you are not," he replies, holding my hand to keep me from moving. "My orders are to keep you safe in the car, and I shall do that. Now, let the others see to the rest. We were expecting this. Trust me."

I freeze and look at him. "Who gave you orders?"

He doesn't answer.

The shots are going on outside, but they have slowed down. I'm dying to know what is going on. I reach over to roll the window down and Skull grabs my arm, *again*.

"I would not do that, querida."

"Well I would. I want to know what is going on! We

can't just hide away in here while the others are risking their lives!" I argue grabbing the gun I had put in the seat beside me. That's when the pain hits. I scream.

"Que te duele, querida?" Skull asks.

"English!" I growl out, because it feels like a vise grip has locked onto my stomach. I feel warm fluid gushing down my legs. My water breaks. It can't break, I'm not far enough along.

"Nicole, what is wrong?" Skull says when I start crying.

"I think my water just broke."

"No jodas!"

Skull starts wadding up his jacket and bracing it at the door, then he slides me against it. I can't really argue because I'm in pain. My eyes are watering and I'm trying to remember how to breathe correctly, but there was never a shower of bullets going on at the Lamaze class. Hell, I only have two classes under my belt. I know next to nothing. Dragon said we had plenty of time, that's just another thing he was *fucking wrong* about.

"Keep the gun trained at the door, and if someone opens it you do not know, shoot."

I want to ask him if it just wouldn't be easier to lock the doors, but the idea of getting to shoot Michael makes me happy—so I don't. Besides, Skull seems a little freaked out. I can understand it, I am too. But he looks a little green, so I'm afraid to question him too much.

I train the gun at the door, trying to breathe in and out when another pain strikes.

"Oh God, another one. That's really close together right? It seems like it's really close together, Skull."

He bends on the floor and I wince because he's leaning where my water broke. There goes his nice suit. I'd be embarrassed, but I'm hurting too much. I train my gun at the door because if it opens, I'm going to shoot first and ask questions later. Michael will not walk away from this breathing.

Skull reaches under my dress and I grab his hand.

"What the hell do you think you're doing?"

"Easy mujer, I am just going to take your underwear off. We need to see what is going on."

"Oh hell no, I don't think so."

"Querida, we need to know," he says as his hand is going back under my dress.

I use my free hand to stop at least one of his hands. I can't get the other one because I'm clutching the gun. I'm starting to panic. There's no way I want Skull to be the one who helps me here. Hell, I want to be at the hospital. It's too soon to have the baby.

"If you want to help, haul your bony, Spanish ass up to the driver's seat and get us to the damn hospital!"

He ignores me and I feel his hand grab the side of my panties and I can't stop the scream that comes out.

"I said, no!"

The door is ripped opened. I grip the gun and tighten my finger on the trigger. I discharge the weapon, before I can register what I'm seeing. I scream out in shock as I focus on the face in front of me.

"What the fuck is going on in here?" Dragon growls.

Dragon. Is he real?

He dodges as the gun goes off, but the bullet still hits him. Skull is watching and as the bullet hits Dragon's flesh, he fills my vision.

His head goes down, "Dios mio mujer, que hiciste!"

I don't know what he said. I just have one word repeating in my head.

Dragon.

Chapter 25

DRAGON

I HEAR NICOLE scream out and then yell, "I said, no!"

I lose my fucking mind. I *trusted* Skull to watch over her. What kind of shit is he trying to pull? When I yank the door open the last thing I expect to see is my woman lying down in the limo seat with Skull bent over and his head between my woman's legs. His hand is up under her dress and I am about to tear the motherfucker's head off. That's when I notice the gun wavering in Nicole's hand and hear the discharge. I dodge the motherfucker, but I'm so close it tears into my upper shoulder. Son of a bitch hurts like fuck, but I ignore the pain and grab Skull by the back of his neck hauling his fucking ass out of the car. He yanks away from me and I let him, turning to my woman. Rage is boiling inside of me.

"What the fuck are you doing?"

Nicole's face is pale as a ghost. She just lays there, breathing hard. *Motherfucker* was Skull that good? I know it's not rational, but you do not see what I just saw and be rational.

"Are you…Dragon is that you?" She asks and I suddenly remember she thinks I am dead. Which would have calmed me the fuck down, except there was a man between her legs.

"Yeah Mama, surprise, it's me. I sure as fuck didn't expect to see you getting it on in the back of a limo, pregnant with my baby, on the day of my funeral, with gunfire every-fucking-where."

She squeaks. Starts to speak and then stops. She awkwardly rolls to sit up, flashing some black silk panties in the process. *I guess I should be thankful she managed to keep them on.* Then she slides out of the car and stands in front of me. I don't know what I expected. A kiss? Her falling into my arms? Something, but I didn't expect her to slap the shit out of me. She's got some power in her hit, too. It rings my jaws.

"How the fuck are you still alive?"

"Gee? I don't know, because I am? That don't explain why Skull had his hands up your dress, Mama."

"Oh my God! Are you being serious with me right now?"

"It don't get much more serious than what I just saw, woman!"

She raises her hand to slap me and I grab it this time. Oh, hell no, that's not happening again.

"Don't you dare slap me again, Mama. I gave you the first one, that's it."

"You gave it to me? Oh my God!" You insufferable...."

I should have been watching, but fuck, days of watching my woman hurt and not being able to hold her have taken its toll on me. The last two nights, I've snuck into her bed after she fell asleep, just to hold her. The way her eyes light up in anger now, grab my attention and I can't look away—even if I tried. Which is a shame because if I had been watching I would have seen her take her free hand, that still has the gun in it, and slam the butt of it into my balls.

Motherfucker.

Skull reaches over and grabs the gun and secures it. I would have done it, but I'm too busy grabbing my nuts and fighting to stand up.

"Did you just fucking punch me in the nuts with a loaded gun?"

"Yes! And I'd do it again if Skull would give me the damn gun back!"

"Woman! You could have shot my dick off!"

"Don't give me any ideas!"

"What the fuck, Nicole? I figured you'd be upset I kept this hid from you, but hell you…"

"If I might interject…"

"Shut the hell up, motherfucker! I'll deal with you in a minute."

"That's all well and good compadre, but perhaps you can finish your fighting for after we get to the hospital."

"The hospital?"

"Well, as you have been shot and Nicole is in labor, it seems to me that would be the place to continue this…discussion, sí?"

"Labor?"

"Oh hell, I shot you," Nicole says.

It's then I notice the way Nicole is holding her stomach.

"Mama, let's get you in the car," I respond, trying to

tap down the anger. I know it was stupid of me to jump to conclusions in the first place. Trouble is, when Nicole is involved I don't think logically.

Before I can help her, she yells, "No! Don't you touch me!"

I freeze and step back from her. She looks around and her eyes stop on Dancer. "You knew, didn't you?"

"Mama, we don't have time for this right now. It's too early for you to be in labor. We need to get you to the hospital."

"Don't you *dare* talk to me, Dragon! It's your fault I'm in labor. What the fuck were you thinking by letting me believe you were dead? Do you have any idea what you did to me?" She cries out and tears are pouring down her face now.

"Damn it, Mama."

We stop, as Bull and some other members pull up outside. Crusher comes out about that same time, and they are all staring at me, like they see a ghost. Probably because to them, I am.

"Bull? Did you know?" Nicole asks.

Bull's eyes lock on mine and his body goes rigid.

"No, I didn't, Little Mama."

Oh fuck no. That is not okay, no one calls Nicole anything close to that. Before I can argue, Nicole speaks up again.

"Will you take me to the hospital?" She asks and I breathe a sigh of relief, thinking she finally has come to her senses.

I take a step towards her and stop when I realize that it's not me she's talking too. *No*, it's *Bull*.

"What's wrong?" Bull asks, getting off his bike.

"My water just broke," she whispers sounding more broken than I remember her being, even when she thought I was dead.

Bull sweeps in and lifts Nicole into his arms, like he's carrying her over a threshold. The sight of it fuels my anger again and I step up to stop this shit and shut it down, when Nailer grabs me by the arm.

"What happened to your arm, man?" He asks, but I know he's keeping me from Bull. I may even understand why, but I don't like it.

"I shot him!" Nicole calls out and those blue eyes I've always loved stare at me with so much anger they freeze me where I'm at. "And if he comes near me again, I'll shoot more than just his shoulder."

I watch as Bull loads Nicole up in his truck. My eyes never leave until the truck is out of my line of sight.

"How the fucking hell are you standing in front of me?" Crusher asks. I turn away, not bothering to answer.

"Nailer, get me to the hospital."

"Answer me, motherfucker, how are you standing here and none of us knew?" Crusher looks around at his brothers thinking they will join in. Trouble is they can't. The only motherfuckers who didn't know I was alive was him and Bull. It doesn't take long for that shit to sink in.

"Oh, I see how it is."

"Do you?"

"What the fuck man? I'm your VP! Bull's your Enforcer! Where the fuck do you get off not letting us know what the hell is going on?"

That's it. I snap. I've gone my limit.

"Tell me, motherfucker, why didn't you bother letting me know what the fuck you were doing? Better yet, did you even try to get a hold of me after our call dropped, to tell me about the damn bomb? Did I know one thing about you killing a prisoner and burying his body? Did you clear *one* motherfucking thing with me?" I growl.

Crusher steps back, "Drag man…"

"While you thought I was dead, man, did you do one thing for this fucking club? Did you takeover in my stead like you were *supposed* to do?"

"Drag you got to understand, she needed…"

"I *don't have to understand* a fucking thing. My woman is pregnant and I still put the motherfucking club first. You're done here."

"Drag, man…"

"You are fucking done. Turn your motherfucking cut in."

"Drag man, we should vote on this," Hawk speaks up.

I turn and look at him. As a full pledged in member he has a right to call for a vote. I could veto it, but I'm too fucking tired to fool with it. I need to get to the hospital to see Nicole. She's way too early in her pregnancy to give birth to our baby and she didn't look good.

"Whatever. Lock him down. I need to get to my woman."

"I'll take you, hermano," Skull says.

I haul off and punch him. It's not as hard as it would have been *if my woman hadn't shot me*, but it still gets my message across.

"What was that for?"

"For having your hands up my woman's dress."

"I was worried about the bebé."

"Yeah, until I see an M.D. after your name, keep your fucking hands to yourself."

With that I turn and get in Nailer's car. I imagined my homecoming a hell of a lot different. Instead, I'm heading to the hospital because my woman *is in labor*. I don't have a woman and I got nothing but a gunshot wound and sore nuts. Welcome home…*yeah right*.

Chapter 26

NICOLE

'M LYING IN a hospital bed, staring up at the ceiling trying to figure everything out and coming up very empty.

Dragon's alive. How can two words flood you with such joy and fill you with white-hot anger all at the same time? He's alive. He lied all this time, and let me think he was dead. He let me *grieve* for him. He let me *hurt*. How do I forgive that? I don't even know why he did it, but I know it was for the club. It's just another example of him putting the club before me. I was *hating myself* because I put Dani first. Why? Apparently it is completely okay to do that. There are no lines you can't cross.

"Mrs. West?" The doctor comes in and Bull stands up. I don't have the heart to correct the doctor with my real last name. I'm too damn tired. I had told the doctor I would be Mrs. West last time we talked. I was wrong—about so many things.

Bull's hand goes to mine. He came back as soon as they dressed me in a hospital gown and got me settled into a labor room. Which is really just a private room in the hospital, equipped for delivery of the baby. I didn't complain, and given that I'm scared to death. It's good having him here with me.

The nurses placed these large bands around my stomach and are monitoring my contractions. They gave me some medicine through a drip to try and stop them. They aren't as frequent, but they haven't stopped. The only reassurance I have is the sound of the fetal heartbeat echoing from one of the machines. I like they are keeping track of the baby's heartbeat. I need that, *and* Bull's hand wrapped securely around mine right now. *It's all I have.* I squeeze him tighter as the doctor looks at me, his face is solemn, so I know the news can't be good.

"I'm afraid we've been unsuccessful in stopping the labor."

Bull caps his free hand over our already joined ones.

"What does that mean?" He asks and I'm glad, because I can't seem to find my voice.

"Realistically, we'd like for your wife to be at least another month along…"

"She's *my* damned wife, not his."

Dragon is standing at the door shooting angry glares at me and Bull. It's okay, because I can give them back; I just have too much to worry about right now. The doctor looks startled. Someone should prepare him, because I have a feeling it's only going to get worse.

"Coming back from the dead must have given you amnesia, because I left your ass at the altar. Please continue doctor." It would appear that with Dragon around, I find my voice relatively easily. It also helps that my anger at him gives me something to focus on, rather than the fear I have for my baby.

The doctor clears his throat, looks back between Dragon, me and Bull nervously, but continues.

"As I was saying, ideally we would prefer you to be another month along, but healthy babies are delivered every day at 28 weeks and above."

My hand goes to my stomach and I rub it gently. I'm terrified. That's probably the only reason I let Dragon come over and place his hand on top of mine, blanketing our child together. Now is not the time for our fight. We need to concentrate on the baby.

With that decision made, I look at the doctor.

"We chose this hospital based solely on the abilities of your NICU and reputation. So, I have to trust you. Doctor?"

"Yes?"

"Will my baby survive?"

"I can't give you surety Mrs. We...Nicole. Based on the ultrasound and records you're at twenty-seven weeks. This means the baby's lungs are developing. He's started producing a substance called surfactant. This will help keep the lungs inflated when he's born. That increases his chances tremendously."

I can't stop the tears that come. It feels like all I've been doing lately is crying, but none have been more terrifying than these. I can't lose my baby. I can't. Up until this point I thought they would be able to stop it. I know that's naïve, I should have known when my water broke, but I was still functioning with hope—you would think after the last two weeks, hope would have fled.

"Nicole, babies are amazing in their resilience. Today, a preemie that was born at twenty-eight weeks is having this G.I. tube removed and eating completely on his own."

His words should bring me comfort, and they do in a way. Still, I picture this tiny baby with tubes and wires and the tears fall again.

"We're going to prepare a surgical room for a cesarean. I know you wanted a natural child birth, but we want the delivery to be as comfortable and stress free as possible for the baby."

"O…okay." I'm doing my best to hold the tears back, but I can't. One hand is grasping Bull's and the other is still allowing Dragon to hold it. I'm weak.

The doctor gives me a kind smile and then leaves. My eyes close; the tears still falling and I try to breathe slowly. I don't want Little Dragon to know I'm upset. I'm sure he's had enough of that lately. Dragon kisses my tears. I want to melt into him and trust him to make it all better, but I can't. I can't trust him. He *betrayed* me. I turn my face away to look at Bull. He squeezes my hand.

I need someone to tell me it will be okay. No one can. So I pray.

I just pray.

Chapter 27

DRAGON

I MAY BE in hell and it's what I deserve. I'm just starting to see how deep the hurt I've brought to Nicole has gone. I did what I had to do for the good of the club. Trouble is picking the club over Nicole, may have caused me to lose her. At the time it seemed like a brilliant plan. Brilliant because I'm fucking stupid.

I needed to shut Kavanagh down, I needed to do it quickly. When Crusher called and said he had Dani, I knew it was just a matter of time before the viper tried to strike again. I wanted him to think he had won. I wanted to lure him into attacking on a day and time of my choosing. It took a lot of work, but losing Frog was the last straw. I had no choice, my club has been going to hell for way too long. I needed to get back to the President I was before Nicole. I've become too relaxed, which implies weakness, and in turn gets people killed. So I made my choice. I pulled in Dancer and Skull and the rest of the crew, and kept Crusher and Bull in the dark because their heads were *not* in the game. *I made that choice.* Crusher has fucked up and gone against my orders too many damned times for me to trust him. Bull? Fuck, I don't even know where his head is at, but I do know as club enforcer, he should have made sure our vehicles were safe and security at the church should have been double what it was. Those are just plain facts. So I made a motherfucking choice I didn't want to. It's what a President does. It's one I should have made sooner and because I didn't, we lost a man—a good man.

Still, making that choice came at a cost. I know it hurt Nicole. I know it tore her heart out. I saw it firsthand. Watching her hurt and grieve tore me up inside. I watched her from a distance, I held her after she fell asleep, all the time repeating in my head that I was making it safe for her and the baby.

I never dreamed the stress could make her go into labor. The doctor said it could have been a number of things, but stress puts her at high risk. This is on me. Did choosing my club cost me my woman and my child? These thoughts keep going over and over in my head while I sit in this damned waiting room. They took Nicole back a few minutes ago. She didn't even talk to me. I look over at Bull. She held his *fucking* hand the entire time. Who the fuck does he think he is.

"You shouldn't be here."

"Nicole wants me here."

"She's upset. She doesn't know what she wants right now."

"Who the fuck has her upset? The way I see it, of the two of us, you're the one who should be gone."

"Motherfucker, that's *my* woman."

"From where I'm sitting a *man* protects *his* woman. He makes sure she always knows she's *his*. He doesn't put her through hell and expect her to be okay with it. That does *not* happen."

I get up. He's saying nothing I've not been thinking, but seeing it and hearing it come from his self-righteous ass is more than I can handle.

"Get up, motherfucker! You want to throw down with me, I'm ready for you. You need to step the fuck away from my woman and let us work this out."

Bull gets up and I get the satisfaction of knowing I'm going to beat his fucking face in. Nailer gets between us and Hawk holds me back at the same time. Six makes sure he keeps Bull back.

"This ain't the place boys. You're going to get thrown out and Nicole needs you here. *Both of you,*" Nikki says.

She's sitting over with Freak, Dancer, Carrie and several other men including Skull and Diesel. Why they are here, I have no idea. I know Nikki's right, but I do not like it. I don't like it at all. Still, I jerk loose from my brother's hold and sit back down—still glaring at Bull.

"If you had done your job as club enforcer, I wouldn't have had to take the steps I did."

"What the fuck are you going on about now?"

"How did someone get to our vehicles to put bombs on them? Mind telling me that shit?"

Bull's eyes narrow and he stands up and walks two feet in front of me before leaning down to speak. "You need to make up your fucking-bi-polar ass. You haven't had me as club enforcer since my accident. I've been baby-sitting women or cleaning up after your ass. You put others in charge of security. Men who are trained in electronics and shit, but not hand to hand. So, don't come after *me* with this shit-baggage now. Your club is a wreck? Look in the fucking mirror."

He's right. I know it—at least partially. Some of the anger leaves me. I bend down, raking my hand over my head and take a deep breath. When I look back up at Bull, maybe he can see the difference in me because his stance relaxes a little.

"Everybody but Bull get out in the hall."

"Drag…"

"*Now* motherfuckers!"

When the room clears and I get shot with a few more death glares, I look up at Bull.

"You're the one who started staying away from the club. How the fuck can I depend on you if you're not there?" I ask the question that's been bothering me from day one.

"Newsflash, Dragon. I'm going through some shit. Doesn't mean I won't be here for the club, when shit goes down. You should know that man."

My lips curl into a half smile. "Newsflash. You're starting to sound like Nicole."

"She's a hell of a woman," he says sitting down beside me and slapping me on the back.

"She sure as hell is. I fucked up bad, man."

"Yeah, you did."

"Thanks for sugar-coating it."

"She'll come around brother, that woman loves you deep."

"She kind of acts like she hates me right now."

"She probably does," Bull returns.

"Jesus, you're just full of rainbows and shit aren't

you?"

"That's me."

"I can't lose them man," I say in an almost whisper, voicing the biggest fear I've ever had in my life. This is worse than when Nicole was shot... much worse. This time our son is with her. This time she hates me. I need to make things right. I need the chance to show her how much I love her and our child.

"I'm going to go get us some of that shit they call coffee around here. Do you want some?" Bull asks.

I look at him, our eyes locking and see the resentment is gone from Bull.

"Black."

"You got it, Pres."

He must have given the others all clear because they slowly begin to fall back in. I barely look up. How long has it been now? Surely we should have heard something by now. Bull comes back in and hands me my coffee. I take a drink and have to fight to swallow it. It tastes like swamp piss. Another twenty or thirty minutes go by before the doctor finally shows up.

"Family of Nicole West?"

All of us stand up. It feels right. We are a family. It even feels good having Bull beside me. This is why I fight to keep the Savage MC together. This right here.

"Nicole and the baby came out of the surgery. The baby is in serious, but stable condition in the NICU. One of his lungs collapsed..."

"Fuck...," I can't stop the word that pops out.

"I'll be honest, Mr. West, I thought we would lose him. Your son is strong however, and he is a fighter. He's holding his own and we have the lung re-inflated. He actually appears farther along than tests showed, which means there's more bone and muscle mass to work with. We just have to take it day by day."

"And Nicole?" I ask, my heart feeling as if it is trying to jump out of my chest.

"She's doing well. She should be out of recovery soon and you can see her. If you follow me I can take you to see your child."

I nod and follow him out. He leads me down the hall and another small corridor and then to the private unit. I put on gloves and a gown that the nurse hands me and then I put a mask over my face. My son is in a square thick Plexiglas tank with circles on one side that are protected and covered by a black rubber-like material. He's so small. I don't think I've ever seen anything so small and he has so many wires and tubes running from him, it hurts to see. I can't touch him. I can't hold him. My hand would almost swallow him. Still, I hear the beating of his heart on one of the monitors and it sounds strong.

My son is a fighter.

Just like his dad, he's a fighter.

Chapter 28

NICOLE

I FEEL LIKE I've been hit by a truck. Everything in me is sore. Worse, I feel empty. After six months of having Little Dragon inside of me, not having him now feels wrong. Shit, I'm so tired of that word—*wrong*. That's Dragon's fault.

All of this is Dragon's fault. He keeps trying to come in and see me. I haven't let him. I know he'll get tired of that soon and just barge in, but for now, I'm thankful he's restraining himself. I haven't even gotten to see my baby, yet. I got to stay awake through the cesarean, so I had a quick glimpse of him—which was good and bad. I thought we had lost him right away, and the terror that struck in my heart still echoes.

I'm told they will take me down to him sometime this evening. I always pictured giving birth and having Little Dragon placed upon my chest; dreamed of being the first one to hold him. *I wanted that.* Dragon took that away from me, too.

I hold my hand up and look at it. I had to take all my jewelry off for the surgery, and I haven't put my engagement ring back on. I can't bring myself to and at the same time my hand feels barren. I miss the feel and weight of it on my finger.

"Where's your ring at, Mama?"

I close my eyes and sigh. I knew this was coming.

"Have you seen the baby?" How bad is it that I can't even bring myself to call him our child. It doesn't feel like I ever had Dragon as a partner. That sounds stupid, but it's exactly what I am feeling.

"I just came from there. He's still holding his own. The doctor said they were bringing you to him in a little while," Dragon answers.

"Yeah, I only got to see him for a minute because of his lung," I reply, staring out the window opposite of Dragon. I don't want to see him right now. Seeing him *hurts*.

"Mama, we have to talk if we're ever going to get past this."

"Some things… you just can't get past."

"We can."

"You let me think you were dead, Dragon. You let me grieve for you, hurt and blame myself. You destroyed me and now you just expect me to forgive you and be grateful you're back."

"I didn't have a choice, Nicole. I did what I had to do for the club, to keep us all safe."

"I'm starting to hate the club."

"Nicole," he sighs and starts again. "Mama…"

"Tell me, Dragon, if you could only save one of us? The club or me? Would I lose out to the club again?"

"Damn it, Nicole! That's not fair. I did what I did to protect what was mine, and that includes you. A man ain't a man, if he's weak."

I close my eyes. I've tried to hold it in, but he's just not letting it go. So I decide to just let him have the cold, hard truth.

"You didn't protect me, Dragon. Because of you, I nearly lost our child. I still might! Because of you? Our child is clinging to life, locked away from me, instead of in my arms; I can't even feed him. A tube gets to feed him! You took so much from me, Dragon, I can't even begin to count it all. So, forgive me if I don't buy that you did it *all for me*."

"What do you want from me, Nicole? People were dying. I had to put a stop to it. I was backed into a corner."

"I don't know, Dragon, maybe letting me in on what you had planned?"

"I had to move quickly, Kavanagh had too many eyes and he needed to believe that you were suffering. He needed to believe he had won. I didn't have any other choice," Dragon says.

That's when I turn to look at him. Can he tell how cold I feel on the inside? I may never be warm again.

"There's always a choice, Dragon. You just pick the one that means the most to you."

"Damn it, Mama!"

"You need to leave."

"Mama..."

"I'm tired, Dragon. Please, just go."

"I'm not about to go until we fix this, Mama. You and I are forever."

I ring the nurse, not bothering to respond.

"Yes, ma'am."

"Could you come here, please?"

"Are you hurting, Mama?" Dragon asks.

In more ways than I could ever tell you. I think it, but I don't tell him. He wouldn't get it.

"Mrs. West?"

"It's actually, Miss Wentworth," I correct her, because right now, that seems extremely important. "Could you escort Mr. West out? I'm just too tired for company and I want to rest up before I go to see my son."

The nurse looks between us confused, but nods.

"Certainly, if you'll just follow me, Mr. West."

"This is not over, Nicole."

"This has been over since the moment you let me think you were gone, Dragon."

"Bullshit," he says and stomps out.

My head goes back against the pillow. I guess I won round one.

Chapter 29

DRAGON

TWO WEEKS OF bullshit. That's what I've gotten from Nicole. Two complete weeks of *bullshit*. She won't see me, she won't talk to me, and except for when we get to visit our son together, I get zero emotion from her. How do I go about fixing things with her if she's not even going to try? Did I kill her love? Why can't she understand that what I did, I did for all of us?

Today, Nicole gets to come home from the hospital. She doesn't really want to. She wants to stay at the hospital with our child, but they are making her. Carrie finally got her to agree to stay at the hospital until the last visitation with Chase, and then come home to rest before going back.

Of course, I didn't get any of that from Nicole. I hear everything second-hand these days. She even named our child without telling me. Chasin Donovan West. Kid will *hate* it. *Fuck*, I hate it. It doesn't matter, he'll get a road name when he's old enough. The fact that I walked into the room to find he had been named pisses me off more than anything else. I let it slide, figuring she was just getting her own back, but I'm getting pretty sick of being shut out. Tonight I'll finally bring her home and we'll start getting this lined out. It can't happen soon enough for me.

I miss having her in my arms and talking to her. I miss just being able to see her every day. Having her away from me, leaves the days empty.

I walk into her hospital room holding her favorite flowers, Peruvian Lilies. She's standing up, putting her stuff in her overnight bag, when I walk in. She freezes, looks at me and back to the flowers. She sighs, and gives me a look like I kicked her dog or something, and then goes back to packing.

"All packed up to come home, Mama?"

"All packed," she whispers, not bothering to look up.

"Do you like your flowers?" I finally ask, because I feel stupid holding them.

"You shouldn't have."

I'm tired. It's been too long since I've had her lips. Maybe I need to remind her what we have together? I place the flowers on the bed and pull her gently to me. She holds herself stiff, but she comes. I wrap one arm around her and use my other to pull her chin up, so she looks at me. There's such sadness in her blue eyes. I want to take it away.

"Mama…" I whisper, staring into her shimmering eyes, getting lost in their depths.

"Dragon, we need to…"

I press my lips against hers, stopping the sentence before she can finish it. My tongue slides into her open mouth. I taste her and groan at the burst of flavor. It's been way too long since I've had this. I forcefully explore the depths of her mouth, owning it. She holds stiff against me for the space of a minute and then slowly melts in my arms. Her arms go around me to hold me close. *God, I've missed that.* Her nails dig into my back and I groan at the pleasure. Six weeks until I can have her. *Fuck,* I'll never survive.

"Mama, I have missed your taste," I say when we finally break apart. She keeps her head down, resting her forehead on my chest. We stand like that for a minute, I'm hoping to hear something from her. One small sign of encouragement. I get nothing but silence.

"Talk to me, Mama. Please, talk to me."

"That shouldn't have happened."

"It definitely should have. It *will* happen—a fuck of a lot more."

She looks up at me then, and I wish she hadn't. The tears are there, hiding in the depths of those blue eyes.

"It can't happen again."

"Whose mark do you have on you, Nicole?"

"It doesn't matter," she whispers and it pisses me off.

"Whose mark, Mama?"

"Yours."

"Do you love me?"

"Dragon…"

"Do. You. *Love*. Me. Woman."

"I always will."

"Then this isn't over," I tell her and she better fucking get that through her head. We will never be over.

"I can't survive loving you again, Dragon."

"What the fuck are you talking about?"

"When I thought you died, my world went dark again. Only it was worse than it had ever been in my past, because now I know what it's like to have love, to feel a part of someone. When you left, you took it all away and left me alone. I can't survive that again."

"I'm right here, Mama. I'm not going anywhere."

"But you did, Dragon. You tore up my world so easily and *you* didn't even stop to think what this plan you made would do. How it would affect me and our child. You made the decision, unilaterally, and you left me alone."

"Mama…"

"You want us to go back, to be what we were. We can't do that, Dragon. I can't be that person with you again."

"Why the fuck not?"

"Because I don't trust you!" I cry. "I don't trust me with you. What if a year down the road something else happens and you, once again, make a decision for the good of the club, to protect everyone, and it leaves me and our child hanging in the wind? How do I know you aren't going to hurt me again? How do I know your decision won't destroy me? Or worse, destroy our child."

"Damn it, Nicole, you make it sound like I wasn't even thinking of you. Part of the fucking reason I did all of this was to protect you and our child. Doing this allowed me to kill that son of a bitch."

"Doing this caused our son to be in a neonatal unit fighting for his life. Did you take into consideration, Dragon, what kind of stress you were putting me under? How you were ripping apart your family, for the good of your club?"

"Damn it, Nicole, I told you the decisions I made were for you, our child and the club."

"And I told you I don't trust that."

"So where does that leave us?"

"Over," she whispers, pulling away from me.

I grab her arm and pull her back to me.

"Don't you say that Nicole, don't you fucking dare say that to me."

"Dragon…"

"You're hurt. I get that, woman. I made the decision and I should have thought it through more, but it's done. I can't go back. I did what I had to do so you and our son didn't end up like Frog. I did what I had to do to protect what is mine, and that means you and Chase."

"His name is Chasin."

"How the hell would I know? You named him without even talking to me, damn it!"

"Gee Dragon, you *died* without consulting me!"

"Then be a pissy-ass-bitch, but don't cut me out of your lives! Don't pull us apart, when we don't have to be. You thought you lost me and I was there! I know it sucked. God Mama, don't you think it was as bad for me, not being able to be with you?"

"That right there! You see!"

"What the hell are you talking about now?"

"It wasn't as bad for you, Dragon! It was nowhere *near* as bad! Do you know why? Because your fucking ass knew I was alive. You knew you would see me again! You knew where I was! You have no idea the hell I went through. You never once put yourself in my shoes."

I pull away and rake my hand over my head.

Fuck this.

"So you'd rather tear us apart than to even try? What

kind of weak-ass shit is that, Nicole? That's not the woman I fell in love with."

She just stands there looking at me. She says nothing. *Nothing.*

I sigh. I'm so tired. I'm tired as hell. I grab the flowers and throw them in the garbage, because apparently that's what I am to her at this point.

"Let's go see our son and get you back to the club."

"I...I'm not going to the club, I..."

"You're fucking what, Nicole?" I ask, my voice sounds as resigned and tired as I feel.

"I'm staying with Carrie and Dancer."

I stare at her. I just stare. Yet another fucking decision made without me. Yet another motherfucking moment in which Nicole shows me I don't factor into her world. Why do I keep fighting it?

"Fine. We'll go see our son and then I'll take you to Dance's."

"Carrie's picking me up..."

"Of course she is. Tell me, is it fun, Mama?"

"What... what are you talking about?"

"Is it fun where you're at? Cutting me up into little pieces and throwing me out with the garbage?"

Her face goes white, but I don't ease up.

"Are you getting some of your own back? Is that what you're doing? Cause, whatever this is, I hope you're getting what you need from it. I get it. I hurt you. I wronged you, so you feel it gives you the right to get back at me. You want me out of your life, Nicole? Fine. You want to do this to us. What-the-fuck-ever. You can have it. I am fucking done. I'm going to see my son. I'm going to go have a fucking drink, maybe the fucking bottle, and I'll leave you the fuck alone, like you seem to be wanting, so badly. So, have fun on your fucking high horse."

I slam the door as I leave. I spend a few moments with Chase. When Nicole walks in, I don't even look at her.

"I'll be back tomorrow, C. Keep fighting," I tell my son and then I leave. I don't look back. Apparently, there's nothing there for me anyway.

Chapter 30

NICOLE

D O YOU EVER wish you could have that one moment back? That one moment when, even if you were in the right, you have the feeling that your decision, your actions or inactions changed the course of your life and fear what might happen?

As Dragon walked out of the room, that feeling swamps me and robs my air. I *lied*. I don't want it to be over. I don't want to live without Dragon. I love him. He loves me. The trouble is, I don't think we love in the same way. He didn't say he was sorry. He put me through hell, and I'm convinced that's a major reason I went into labor. Then he accuses me of doing something wrong with Skull, on the day of his funeral! In the back of the limo, on the way to the cemetery with gunfire everywhere! I'm owed a freaking apology somewhere in that. He should be down on his knees begging for forgiveness and kissing my feet. Not making me feel like total shit (which he did) and walking out on me.

So, instead of following my first instinct and running after him, I watch him leave. If he doesn't try to make things truly right, there's nothing I can do. The acknowledgment of that sours in my stomach. I can't help it. I have more than just me to think about now; I have Dominic.

I didn't name our baby Chasin Donovan like he thought. I named our child Dominic West. No middle name; it wasn't needed. I want him to have the same exact initials as Dragon, and I wanted a strong name, that's true. Still, Dominic was Frog's real name and I thought Dragon would like to remember the name of a brother who gave everything for the club. It seemed fitting. Dragon despised the name Chasin when we were going through the book, so, I had the hospital put that name on the card in his room. It was stupid, childish, and immature and I feel like a bitch now, but when the hospital said they needed to send papers off to name our child, I was stuck. If Dragon knew I named his son after someone in the club he would view it as me giving in and I couldn't let that happen. I'm weak. It's taking all I have to hold Dragon off. If he really comes at me, I'm not sure I can resist. Still, I need to fix it.

"Your mommy is a silly, silly woman sometimes, Dom. I promise to try and do better. You'll love your daddy. He's a good man and he'll always take care of you."

I lay my head on the glass of my son's incubator. I hate that word. My son is a human not an animal a farmer is trying to produce. I swallow as I see how small he is next to my hand. It doesn't even seem like he could breathe being so small. You can still see small red lines on his body where his skin is so frail. His head has this dark black hair though. I am not sure what I expected, but that wasn't it. His little features are so wrinkled and small, they're hard to make out because of the wires he has to have monitoring him and the tube they have coming from his mouth. The nurse explained each one and its purpose, but honestly, it goes over my head at this point.

"It'd be nice if you would let Dragon hear you say that," Bull says from the door. His large figure is draped in the yellow hospital gown and the gloves look too tight for his hands, and I can tell he's upset with me.

"I know."

"If you know, why did he look like he'd lost every hope he had in the world when I saw him leaving?"

"Because I told him it was over."

Bull makes that sound he has. It's between a growl and a groan of disapproval. It sounds like the noise a bear makes when he's annoyed he has to run after his food. (Okay, so I watch a lot of Discovery Channel.)

"I don't suppose you bothered to tell him Dom's real name either, did you, Nic?"

Now I know he's pissed, because recently he has taken to calling me Little Mama and odd as it is, I miss it.

"Not yet..."

He fingers the place card on the end of the incubator.

He looks straight at me and his dark eyes pin me. I can feel his disappointment and I don't like it.

"You know I got nothing in the world but love for you, Little Mama, but you're going to have to let go of some of this anger. If not for you, then for Dom. He's what is important."

I break away from his eyes and watch my son, and whisper the one thing that hurts me more than anything else.

"He let me think he was dead, Bull. He destroyed me.

My son is here fighting for his life and I can't help but feel that it's Dragon's fault."

"Nic, I love you, but that's bullshit."

"It's not. Stress…"

"Stress can do a lot, I'm not saying you're wrong. What I am telling you is that things happen the way they are meant to happen. You can't pinpoint one thing that started this. If you want to blame anyone, blame Kavanagh—may his soul rot in hell."

I swallow, because he's right in a way. Still, I resent the way he's laying this at my feet.

"He shouldn't have locked me out, Bull. He shouldn't have done that to me. He let me think he was dead!"

"I'm not saying he was completely right either, Nicole. I'm saying what you're doing isn't making it any better."

"He didn't even apologize!"

"Nicole, how many women do you think Dragon let in as far as you've gotten? Hell, even a fourth of the way?"

"I don't want to think of Dragon with another woman."

"None."

"Bullshit."

"I'm not talking fucked, Nicole."

I look around the room, luckily the nurse that stays with Dom has left while I'm here, but still…

"Don't use that word around Dom."

Bull looks up at the sky like he's praying for divine intervention and shakes his head. "That boy will know what fuck means before his tenth birthday. Probably much sooner. Accept it now, woman."

"Doesn't mean I can't fight it, Bull."

"Lord have mercy."

"For someone that doesn't talk a lot, you sure are getting chatty."

"I like you."

I smile.

"He hurt me bad, Bull. He even accused me and Skull of getting it on in the limo at his damned funeral! Which was fake, anyway!"

"Nic…" he starts and his voice cracks and he starts again. "Nicole, Dragon has never let another person in, except you. He even keeps his brothers at a distance. He's going to fuck up. You want him, you're going to have to show him. He ain't going to know on his own, besides, you women can be crazy."

"He was wrong."

"Are you willing to throw away what you two have? Your son's *family* for the sake of being right?"

"I'm not giving in on this and letting Dragon off the hook, Bull. I can't spend my life letting him have his way in everything. He has to know what he did was wrong, on so many levels."

"So, don't give in completely, but being childish isn't helping."

"I'll change the damn name!" I yell ripping the card up. "I had planned on doing it before you got here anyway," I say grumbling.

Bull halfway smiles.

I go over to where I watched the nurse hand me a card last time. She refused to write Dom's fake name for me. I had to do it. (I might have mumbled she was a self-righteous bitch, under my breath.) I write Dominic West on the paper and put it in the place card holder on the incubator. (Again, I *hate* that word.)

Bull stays a little longer. I'm grateful for the company. He finally gets up to leave; as he walks to the door he stops and turns back around to look at me.

"Nicole? Does anyone win if you don't give in a little?"

"I…"

"Just think about it. I'll check on you soon."

He leaves. I'm left wondering how to get over the anger and resentment I have inside of me. I don't really have an answer.

Chapter 31

DRAGON

"DRAGON MAN, THE men are starting to ask questions," Dance says coming into the main room of the club.

I'm sitting at the bar, doing what I've done almost every day for the last week; ever since my run-in with Nicole. Life doesn't suck as bad if you're drunk off your ass through most of it. Dance sits beside me and I wish he'd fuck off.

"About what?" I say downing another shot.

"Shit, man, everything. You've not even had the vote about Crusher. The whole fucking place is in limbo."

"Fuck the club. It's already cost me too much. You can have it. There, problem fucking solved."

"It hasn't cost you shit. You haven't even got off your drunk ass to go see your son in over a week. You haven't been by to check on your woman. Not once man, that shit is wrong."

"I check on my son," I argue, because that shit needs to be shut down. The rest of it can go to hell.

"You call, you've not seen him one time, Drag. You and me? We know more than most how cold that shit is.

Your boy needs you."

"Nicole is there."

"So? What the hell man, did you lose your fucking balls in that explosion?"

I don't answer him. Instead, I stare at my glass, contemplating another shot. What I don't tell him, what I can't tell him? Is simple. I can't see Nicole and not touch her. I can't handle the hate in her eyes, her coldness towards me. It's just something I am not strong enough to survive again. If that makes me weak, whatever. It's just another reason the club is in better hands with Dancer.

"Fuck it. You want to drink yourself into a bottle, do it, but don't blame me if you lose any chance with your woman."

Dancer walks off. I should celebrate. So I down another shot. How many does that make? It's a little fuzzy.

"He's right, you know."

I turn at the quiet voice from the hall. Dani looks around the room carefully, and then slowly makes her way to the bar when she sees everyone has left. I've seen very little of her since things have gone down. The Dani of today is not the same bitter bitch; she's afraid of her damn shadow. She wears clothes so baggie that you could fit three of her in them. Her hair is down and around her face, and the long sleeves hide her hands, completely. If I could bring Kavanagh back and kill the mother fucker again, I would. Only this time I'd shoot his dick off first, because I don't know what went down while he had Dani, but this woman screams of being raped.

"Right about what?" I ask, not looking at her, because even drunk I know she hates it when people look at her now.

"You need to wake Nicole up, prove to her you want her."

"I've tried, she's the one that sent me packing, D, not the other way around."

"She's hurt. All her life people have overlooked her, forgotten her, or just decided shit for her. You had to know what you did would hurt her."

"What do you suggest?" I can't believe I'm asking her for advice, but I figure she knows Nicole better than anyone, apparently even me.

"It's time to grovel, big boy," she says and I can almost see a flash of the old Dani, and shit, who knew that I would actually miss her.

"Grovel?" I ask putting my shot glass down.

"Beg, crawl, plead…surely those aren't totally foreign words to you, Dragon."

"Pretty damn close," I admit honestly.

"Start with sending her flowers and a note saying you're sorry you are an idiot."

"An idiot?" I ask.

"What else do you call letting your pregnant wife think you were dead and then accusing her of having sex in a limo with another man?"

"I didn't accuse her of that shit," I argue holding my head down, because I know I'm wrong. I hadn't even thought about it really, but in a way, I guess I did. I didn't mean it, it was just the shock of opening the door and seeing that shit, and on top of all the other crap that had just gone down…*Fuck.*

"Get to work, Dragon. Don't let me down, I need to

believe there's at least one good man left in this world," she says getting up and walking carefully back towards the hall. She's still not walking great, she has so many scars on her; it's not funny, but I think the biggest ones are where people can't see them. "You might think about cutting Zander some slack too, Dragon."

"I don't think so." *Yeah, that's not going to happen.*

"Everyone messes up, Dragon, apparently even you," she says and then leaves.

It appears I need to grovel. I think I'll start with a damn shower.

A COUPLE HOURS later, I'm sober as hell. I can tell by the way my head is pounding. Still, I make it to the hospital in time for the last visitation time with my son. I thought Nicole would be there, but she's not.

"Where's my…where's Nicole?" I ask the nurse on duty.

"She called in, apparently she has a fever. She's not allowed to visit with Dom like that. His immune system is too weak."

I nod, absently thinking of Nicole sick. Then I hear what she called baby C. She must have him confused with another kid. I guess it happens, but I don't especially like it. I walk over to sit down by him. There's a lot of changes just in a week. He's still so tiny, but even I can tell his color and other things are better. I wish like hell we could take those damn wires and tubes out. I reach my hand in to place my finger against his tiny palm. He tries to wrap his around it, he can't, but the slight movement makes me smile." I look down at the note card in front of his case-like thing. They call it an incubator, but I don't really care for that term.

Dominic West.

My heart stutters. She named our baby after one of my men. It's a good name, a really fucking good name. It's one I would have picked. Nicole had to know I would. Why did she change it? I want to ask, but right now just knowing she did is enough. I sit and talk with my son the rest of the time, apologizing for being an asshole and promising to do my best to get his family back together. I missed the little guy. How does someone so small own all of you even before he takes a breath?

I'm too wound up when I leave the hospital. I need to check on Nicole. I know she might not want to see me, but I know Dance and Carrie are spending the weekend at Dance's mom's house. I don't want her to be alone and sick. I run by the store and pick up some Sprite and canned soup, store it in my bags and head out.

I pull into the driveway thinking back to that first day I met Nicole. Her sassy mouth and the way she put those barely there shoes on her feet. As I walk towards the small paved step, in front of the kitchen door, groceries in hand, I recall that first kiss…that first taste of her. The way her ass felt in my hands, the way her mouth attacked mine and her breath against my skin. The woman owned me from that minute on and not one second since then have I ever wanted anyone else. She's *it* for me. *Fuck*, she always will be.

I knock on the door, wondering if she will answer it. She had to have heard my bike. I'm about to give up and leave, when it opens. Nicole is standing there with her hair a mess, her eyes watery, her nose red and her face flushed. She's wearing a giant gray t-shirt that comes to her knees that says, *Country Till I Die* on it—which really doesn't sum her up at all. I smile as I take in the shaggy socks on her feet. Some things never change.

"Dragon? Is everything okay?" She asks, surprised to see me.

I feel like a fool for standing there and I'm unsure of what to say, so I hold up the Sprite and the bag I'm carrying, like a dumb ass.

"I thought you might be hungry."

She freezes for a minute and looks at me. She's studying me, I'm not sure for what. I hope she finds it. I need for her to find something in me she wants.

"The thought of food makes me cringe, but I wouldn't mind some Sprite. My stomach is a mess," she says backing away from the door.

I feel like I've won a victory, just being able to get through the door. I hope like hell I get the chance to win another one.

Chapter 32

NICOLE

THE LAST THING I expected to see was Dragon standing at my door. I'm sick as a dog, I can barely breathe, I'm depressed because I couldn't see the baby tonight and I look like hell. When I opened the door and Dragon was standing there, part of me wished a giant hole would swallow me up. I would have rather looked good, but I feel so bad I can't drum up the energy to do anything about it.

I've missed him. Is it possible to be mad at someone and want to kill them, yet hurt from being away from them? It feels like a piece of me is missing, and I don't have the strength to turn him away tonight. Instead, I stand back and open the door wider. He comes in with a lopsided grin, but it has none of the cockiness that Dragon usually has. He goes into the kitchen, finds a glass and puts some ice in it, before filling it with soda.

His large hand brushes my forehead as he hands me the glass.

"You're burning up, Mama," he whispers and his breath fans my hair. I close my eyes, absorbing his touch. God, I miss him.

"It's just a cold."

He kisses the top of my head and my heart literally hurts. It's an exquisite pain.

"Have you taken anything to bring the fever down?"

"I was getting ready to."

"I'll get it. You go lay down on the couch."

"But…"

"Do it, Mama. Let me take care of you tonight, please? No strings, I just need this."

Something about the look on his face and the change in his tone, grabs my attention. I nod and go back into the living room. I curl up in one corner with an afghan over me and take another drink, before sitting it down.

In a little while Dragon comes in the living room carrying a tray.

"Dragon, I told you. I'm just not hungry."

"We'll try and get a little down you. You don't want to get sicker. Dom needs you."

I freeze. Dragon hadn't really been back to the hospital since I put Dom's real name up.

"I didn't realize you knew," I say and I'm thankful for my fever because I probably would have flushed with guilt otherwise.

"I just found out, why did you change it?"

Confession time. Who said confession was good for the soul? Because they're stupid. Still, I might as well bite the bullet.

"It always was Dominic. I was mad at you and I knew you hated those names," I shrug.

"It's a good name."

"I'm really sorry about Frog. His sister seemed to be

having a hard time."

"Yeah, she is. He was all she had."

"We should reach out to her," I tell him, totally ignoring that I'm already putting us back together in my brain.

"Believe it or not, Skull has."

Interesting, but I find myself hoping that works out.

"I'm sorry I was childish. I should have told you the baby's name."

"I was stupid, so I figure you had a right to be childish."

My eyes must have given away my surprise, because he smiles sardonically and then shakes his head.

"I knew better, Mama. You'd never betray me. I was scared you were hurt and opening the door to see what...," he shakes his head. "My big mouth just reacted first and my brain didn't catch up. I'm sorry."

It's silent now and more than a little awkward. I move the spoon around. I manage to get down a spoonful or two of the soup, but that's about it. Dragon gives me that look, so I put the tray on the coffee table and compromise by showing him I'm eating a handful of crackers.

He shakes his head, but his lips curve into a mocking smile. It's a good smile, his eyes crinkle at the corners.

"I'm sorry I shot you," I say when I finish eating and go back to just my Sprite.

His smile grows. His eyes light up. Have I mentioned how much I love his eyes?

"I can't believe you shot me."

"I may need to take gun classes."

"*Oh, hell no.* You could have shot off my balls that last time. I think you need to stay away from guns—for everyone's safety."

"That wouldn't happen if I were trained," I defend.

"We'll see. Here take some ibuprofen and let's see about getting your fever down," he semi-orders, reaching to the forgotten tray to give me the medicine.

I take it and turn back to the TV.

"I remember the first night I came here and you were covered up in that afghan."

My eyes lock back on his.

"I had no idea then just how much you would rock my world, woman. I just knew, I needed you like my next breath."

"Dragon…"

"That's even truer today, Nicole. I might be an idiot, Mama. I know I've cut you deep. I'll try and fix it, but you need to know that I love you with everything I am and if I fuck up, it's not because I don't care."

"Dragon, what's happened to you? You're getting practically mushy, better watch it, you're losing badass-biker status," I try to joke because his words touch me. They're not enough, but they do smooth over some of the hurt, and I'm too sick tonight to try and shore up my defenses against him.

"I'm pretty sure that happened when I let your fine ass talk me into putting on that fucking monkey suit."

"Ugh. If I'm honest, you look damn good in a suit, but I missed my man in his jeans and cut."

"Thank fuck."

It was my turn to smile, which wasn't easy because I was trying to breathe through my mouth.

"My head is woozy."

"Come here and lay in my lap and watch TV. Try to nap, you've run your system down trying to be everywhere, so soon after having surgery."

"I should call and check on Dom."

"He's fine baby, I just came from there, remember? Our boy is a fighter."

"Dragon…"

"I'm not asking for nothing, Mama. Well, that's not true, I'm asking for a chance to prove to you I get what you're saying. That I will do better, but for tonight just let me be close to you and take care of you."

I should tell him to leave, that what he wants is dangerous. I should tell him there is a lot of trust to rebuild. I can't. I'm too tempted. So I twist and turn to my side, laying my head on his lap. My eyes go to the television, but I'm not really watching. The sound is so low, you can barely hear it anyway. In a minute I feel Dragon's fingers comb through my hair and my eyes close at the pleasure of it. I have missed his closeness so much. I had faced the rest of my life without him and, until this moment, I never allowed myself to contemplate ever having him back. The force of emotions that hit me cause moisture to gather in my eyes, but I choke it back. I can't deal with any of that right now.

"Don't blame me if I drool all over your jeans or if you get sick," I mutter, annoyed with myself for being weak.

"It's worth it, just to have you close. I've missed the hell out of you, Mama."

"You sure aren't sounding like the Dragon who thought I'd be the perfect Twinkie to add to his collection."

"That Dragon was a stupid prick. Luckily the taste of your lips, woke my ass up quick."

"So, you admit that's what you wanted from me?" I prod with a giggle, because he's always denied it.

"Just until I had a taste of you. From that moment on, you were *mine*."

"I'm pretty sure you can't own people, Dragon."

"I disagree, you've pretty much owned me from that first day, Mama."

I smile and close my eyes, enjoying the feel of his fingers and the sweetness of just having him here with me.

"Where do you think we would have been, if we hadn't met that day at the gas station?"

"I probably would have been hooked up with Lips and felt empty as hell."

"Lips?" I ask and try to tap down the twinge of jealousy that flairs. (It might be a *big* twinge.)

"She was a Twinkie, but different from the rest. I respected her. We got along well enough, I had been thinking on it. Just never really cared enough to make a move."

"Well...that sounds...fun."

"I didn't want to be that man."

"That man?"

"That sixty-year-old who was still sharing women with his brothers and crawling between the open legs of some chick, not because she gave a fuck about me, but just because she wanted to make it with a member of the Savage crew."

"Wow, Dragon, you paint a pretty picture."

"Mama, until you came into my life, I never realized what happiness was, let alone love."

I soak in those words. I drink them in *deep*.

"Are you feeling okay after the surgery?" He asks softly.

"Yeah, sore and stuff, but they tell me that's normal. All things considered, I'm doing really well."

"My woman's a fighter, it's where our son gets it."

"I figured that trait was pure stubbornness. That is definitely a West family trait, sweetheart."

"I like that," he says after a few minutes of silence.

"What?"

"West family. Hated that fucking name my whole life until you gave it a reason."

Okay so maybe a few tears fall when he says that, but it'd take a stronger woman than I am *not* to react to that.

"I'm getting sleepy…" I say because I am. I just hate to see this evening end.

"Then rest, Mama, I'll lock up and take care of you."

"I'm really glad you came by tonight, Dragon."

"Dani talked me into it."

The mention of Dani's name hurts me. In some ways I've been a lot angrier with her than I have Dragon. Even so, I've still been worried about her.

"How is she?"

"Scarred, and I'm not talking about anything visible, but she was worried about you. She gave me the kick I needed to pull my head out of my ass."

I think about what he just said. I need to talk with Dani and make things better. I just don't think I can right now. I need to work through some of this anger I have inside of me. Still, I promise myself that I will try talking to her soon. I don't want to be cut out of her life.

"I'm glad."

"Me too. Now rest, Mama."

"Yes, Daddy."

"Never thought I'd like that…"

I smile, "What's that?"

"A woman calling me, Daddy. With you, it's hot as hell though. Only thing that would make it better is if you said it while I was smacking that ass of yours."

"Seems like I've heard that somewhere before…" I whisper.

The last thing I hear before sleep claims me is Dragon laughing. *God, I love him.*

Chapter 33

DRAGON

HAVEN'T SLEPT. Since the moment I made the decision to trap Kavanagh—I haven't slept. A nap here, a nap there and that's it. There was no use for me to go to bed unless it was to jack off to thoughts of my woman. Sleep wouldn't come, it mocked me. It didn't take long before I couldn't even cum to the thoughts of my woman, because I was seeing all too well how much she was hurting and that shit was *my* fault. So having her talk and laugh with me again, like we did last night, is the best motherfucking gift I have been given since my son was born. Falling asleep with Nicole laying on her side and my arm pulling her back into me and her hair falling against my chest, just listening to her breathe is a motherfucking miracle. Something about it being the first bed I slept with her all night in… Seems *right*, like we've come full circle. So, for the first night in forever, I actually slept. To be honest, waking up seems like a bad idea; last night was a dream I've had for far too long.

Here I lie, with my eyes closed, willing myself into going back to sleep, and it just doesn't work.

"We're not going there, so you need to tell Dragon, Jr.

to quit poking me in the back," Nicole mumbles and I smile.

"Morning, Mama."

"How'd we get up here?"

"I carried you, after I wiped the drool off my leg."

"I warned you."

"That you did. How are you feeling?"

"I'm not sure. I just woke up because there was a steel rod poking me."

"Hey, I can't help what you do to me, Nicole. It's beyond my control."

"Well you need to tell him to stop, because even if I could—which I can't, we're not going there."

"You could suck him. I'll give you my cum."

"You're so delusional," she says but I can hear the smile in her voice.

"How about you lay in bed and I bring you some breakfast and meds? While you call and check on Dom, sound like a plan?"

"Umm…you're going to cook?"

"Fuck no, I was going to run out to the Truck Stop and pick up two breakfast platters. That way Carrie and Dance still have a kitchen when they get back."

"Ick. Please no."

"Still no appetite? We have to fix this, Nicole. I need you to keep your ass."

She turns and looks at me over her shoulder, like I'm nuts.

"Have you seen my ass? I'm pretty sure there's plenty of it back there."

"I dream of your ass, of sliding my cock in it and fucking it hard. Sinking so deep inside you taste me...."

"Dragon, quit trying to get me horny. I can't have sex yet, damn it, and even if I could you and I are nowhere near that place yet."

I curl closer to her and prop myself up on my arm, so I can whisper in her ear.

"Am I making you horny, Mama?"

"Fuck you."

I grin, as my hand goes over her breasts.

"Shit, I'm going to miss these..."

"Oh my God, Dragon, I'm still a freaking double D cup, even without the milk."

I fake a longing sigh. "I know, it will be like you've let my play toys waste away to nothing."

"Okay, I need to pump and then I'm getting away from you and jumping in the shower. I wouldn't say no to toast and more Sprite."

"Pump?"

"I use a breast pump so they can give Dom the milk. Of course, I'll have to throw it out for a few days because I'm sick."

"They feed him your milk through some of those tubes and things?"

"Yeah. They say it's healthier for him."

"What happens while you're sick?"

"They have donors to provide milk or formula. Now, if you're done questioning me? Toast, Sprite? Remember?"

"No OJ?"

"Afraid to try it."

"Okay. It's yours. Would you like to ride with me to see Dom this morning if your fever's gone?"

"I'm afraid…I don't want to get him sick."

"You can wear a mask and suit up in all that garb. You don't have to touch him, just see him. Come on Mama, I've missed having you on the back of my bike."

I'd been taking a vehicle everywhere, because I didn't want her on my bike when she was pregnant. It will feel good having her there again.

"I've missed it, too…but to be honest, I'm still real sore. Can we take the car?"

I only know a moment of disappointment, because she's not insisting I leave her alone today.

"Anything you want, Mama."

She gives me a strange look but goes on to the shower. I throw my shit on and hit downstairs. I search Carrie and Dance's bathroom and find enough shit so I'm ready to roll, and then go out into the kitchen to fix Nicole's toast. I toast half a loaf and manage to make four pieces that aren't burnt to a crisp. Dance really should invest in a better toaster, those settings are fucked up. Then I set about foraging around and finding me something to eat.

Nicole comes down a little later. She's wearing blue jeans and a silky blue top that matches her eyes. Her long hair is hanging down straight. *Have I mentioned how she takes my breath away?* I love this woman. How in the hell did I get to be the lucky son of a bitch she gave her heart to? I have to find a way to get her to trust me again.

"What the hell are you eating?" She asks, her face is priceless.

"A Twinkie. Found them in the cabinet. I haven't had one in a long time. They're dangerous. They have carcogenical things in them." I say plopping the rest of the cake in my mouth.

"You are a regular laugh a minute today, aren't you?"

I grin and lean back in the chair. I like that I make her smile.

"How's the fever?"

"It seems to be gone," she answers.

"So we're a go for the hospital?"

She looks at me for a minute and my heart stalls. I might have pushed too hard, too fast. I prepare myself for rejection when she surprises me.

"I'd like that," she whispers and she reaches out and takes my hand.

IT'S LATE BY the time we get back from the hospital. I talked her into grabbing a bite to eat with me and the sun is starting to set by the time we get back to Dancer's. She turns at the door and I can already tell she's going to ask me to go home...alone. I bite back the demand on my tongue. I have to proceed carefully, I know that. I can't take her shutting me out again.

"Hey Mama, you look sad, what's wrong?" I ask when I notice there's moisture in her blue eyes.

"I hate leaving Dom. I want him to be okay. I need for him to be....I want to bring him home. I can't even feed him..." She whispers, her voice breaking.

My hand goes under her chin and I pull her in by our still joined hands.

"He'll be home where he belongs soon, Mama. You

heard the doctor this morning. He's getting stronger every day."

"I…know. It's just after having him as a part of me for so long, it all feels empty now. I want to hold him, Dragon, feed him and rock him to sleep. Just *be* a mom to him."

I kiss her forehead, because I don't know what else to say to that. She should have all those things. Hell, we both should. I don't like leaving Little D behind any more than she does.

"It's been a good day, Dragon," she says when we pull apart, but she still holds my hand.

"Let me come in, Mama. Don't send me home without you."

Her tongue darts out to run along the bottom of her lip and her eyes freeze on mine. I've never been the type of man to ask. I've never been the type of man to wait on a woman, but Nicole is not just *any* woman. She's mine.

"Dragon, I…I need to think about things. I'll see you tomorrow, okay? At the hospital?"

I want to scream no. I don't. I pull her in one last time, then let go of her hand to slide mine along the side of her hips. I let my fingers travel under her shirt so I can feel her skin. I need that touch to sustain me. She is, and always will be, my drug of choice.

"Tomorrow then Mama, if that's what you want." I whisper against her lips and then slowly kiss her. Not giving her my passion, but trying to show her how much love I have for her. I need her to know that she is….everything.

When the kiss finally ends she studies me closely then,

breaks away to go inside. I stand there until I see the upstairs light come on.

"Everything been okay tonight?" I call out into the night.

Nailer and Hawk come around from each side of the house.

"Yeah Boss, no signs of anything," Hawk responds.

"You really expecting trouble?" Nailer asks.

"Can't be sure, but I want my woman protected at all times. So you yahoos look alive."

"You got it," Hawk says as they go back into position.

I go climb on my bike, trying to figure out how to get my woman home. I could be totally wrong, but I think when Daddy Kavanagh learns his son is missing he's going to be looking for him. I need to be prepared and that means having my family close.

Chapter 34

NICOLE

I AM EXHAUSTED. Between fending off Dragon's increasingly sexual advances the last several weeks and being here at the hospital twenty-four seven, I'm drained. The bright spot of everything is that Dom is being moved to a regular crib tonight. If he manages to stay warm and do okay in it for a couple of nights, I get to bring him home. He's grown so much, but he's still smaller than any baby I've seen. Last night a baby died that had been in the incubator beside Dom. My heart broke for Sarah—the mom. She was a single parent and had zero support. I gave her my number, I'm hoping she'll stay in touch, but I'm afraid seeing Dom may be too much for her.

Dom is doing so good now. I get to hold him and feed him. I breastfeed before I go home, and we use my milk in bottles during visiting hours. I don't like using the bottles, so I've thought about breastfeeding all the time, but Skull, and even that guy Diesel, is still around and they pop in all the time. I'm pretty sure Dragon would kill both of them if they walked in while I was breastfeeding. Especially since I haven't even let Dom feed in front of him.

It's weird; I'm nervous around Dragon now. I don't

know how to act sometimes. I love him. I want to fix what is between us, but I'm afraid, terrified actually. He promises I don't have to worry about him ever doing something like this to me again. He tells me he's sorry, but I don't think he gets how deeply he wounded me. In the back of my mind I can't help thinking he will keep something else from me. Or worse, he'll just make a decision, do it and not tell me, and leave me and Dom alone, on our own. My brain is a jumble of emotions when it comes to Dragon, and I can't trust myself around him. Ever since the doctor cleared me for sex, I have been pushing him away. I crave him and if I don't keep him at a distance? I'm going to give in. It's a miracle I haven't already. I watch as he leans down and kisses Dom's head. It's a beautiful picture. This strong badass biker covered in tats and wearing a leather cut, bending down and being so delicate with his son. I wish I had a photo of it; Dom needs to see that. I vow to take a picture of it soon, so I can put it up in Dom's nursery, whenever I move out of Dance and Carrie's house. I should have already been looking for a place, but there just never seems to be enough time. Plus, every time I mention it Dragon goes a little crazy. He doesn't understand why I won't come home. I'm not even sure I understand. I do know the reasons are all summed up in one word. *Fear*.

"You ready to go, Mama?"

"Go?" I ask, because I drove here. I'm not sure what he's got up his sleeve now, but again the word *fear* comes to mind.

"I thought we could go look at cribs for Dom and fix his room up at the club."

Oh boy.

"Uhh…Dragon I'm bringing him home with me….to Dancer and Carrie's."

Dragon's face goes solid, like I'm watching and it turns to stone—granite even. You can just see this mask of hardness come over him.

"Let's go. We'll talk in the car."

"Dragon, I drove here."

He walks to me and pulls me from the chair I'm sitting in so I am standing in front of him. He leans in and whispers into my ear, and I get chills. These, however, have nothing to do with sexual awareness. He's mad— *really mad.*

"I'm not fighting in front of my child. Dom will not hear his parents going at each other. But listen to me, Mama, and listen *well.* We *will* have this out. We *will* be talking about this and there is no motherfucking way my son is going to another man's house when he leaves here. Now get your shit and let's get out of here."

I get my stuff and think I might be in shock, because I should be ready to cut his balls off, but instead, I'm aroused as hell. It has to be hormones still running amuck. Surely, that's it? I mean, I haven't had sex in like over three months, hell maybe four, the time is starting to blur. I follow Dragon down to the parking garage. I say follow, because there's no way I can keep up with this stomping-mad, long-legged, jackass. I'm about out of breath just trying.

When we get down there, I start to go to my car and Dragon grabs my arm and steers me to his instead.

"Dragon, you can't just tell me what to do!" I gasp,

but he has the passenger door open and is lifting me up and sitting me in the seat, before I can even blink. He reaches around, buckles me in and I sputter trying to form coherent words when he slams the door—in my face.

He climbs in on his side, starts up the car and heads out on the main road.

"Dragon! I can't just leave my car there! Besides, I have things to do to make sure Dom's room is ready."

He doesn't answer, instead he reaches for his phone.

"Yo, Bull? Can you have one of the boys pick up Nicole's car at the hospital? Yeah man. We'll vote on it at Friday's church. Later."

"What did you do?"

Silence.

"Damn it, Dragon! You answer me right now or I'll…"

"Shut it, Mama."

"*Shut*…listen, I've had enough. You can't just…"

He swerves the car, pulling over to the side of the road and slams it into park. It comes to a stop with a groan, and he cuts the engine.

"You want to have this out here, Mama? Fine, we'll have it out here. How about the fact that I've let you lead me around by my dick long enough, and you are going to get this fucking knot out of your ass once and for all!"

I look at him like he's insane, because I think he is. I unlatch my seat belt then open the door and jump out. Screw this, I'll walk home.

I don't get but just a few steps before he's pulling me back to him. I try to fight him, to break free, but it's impossible.

"What the fuck are you doing?" He barks.

"Walking home!"

"Fuck, woman, you haven't been home in months!"

I stop fighting him and go still. He doesn't let me go, but his hold loosens.

"You took that from me."

He lets go and turns me around to face him. It's dark and I can barely make out his face. A car goes by and its headlights highlight his features, briefly. I can see nothing but the confusion etched there.

"Nicole…"

"You took it all. You took safety. You took my heart and crushed it. You took happiness. You took my *fucking* air, Dragon. You cut my chest open, yanked my heart out and threw it on the ground! All I could do was stand there, looking at it and *bleed*. Alone! *You did that!* Now you think I can just put that away and everything will be fine! Gee! Wow! Look here! I'm not dead! *Just kidding!* I had to do it honey! I had to do what was best for you and the club! It's all better now! You know what Dragon? *Fuck you!*"

I've lost it. Tears are pouring down my face and it pisses me off even more because I don't want to cry more over this man. I've cried fucking rivers, and he thinks I've just got a *knot in my ass*?

"What the fuck did you expect me to do, Nicole? The bastard had me by the balls. He was taking pot-shots at us. I just lost a man. A man I *liked*. A man I respected. My woman left me standing at the fucking altar with a fucking monkey suit on. My best friend had flown the coop. I had to make a quick decision. I had to take control and be the fucking man I was before you. The fucking man I *still* am,

Nicole. I had to go on the attack or he was going to hurt you, hurt our baby. I didn't have much of a fucking choice. I did what I'm trained to do, damn it. I went to war. Hit him, when he didn't think I could."

"You left me alone, Dragon. You took…you took my world," I whisper brokenly.

Chapter 35

DRAGON

MY WOMAN IS standing in front of me, tears pouring down her face and finally that cold shell she's encased herself in has started to crack. While I hate the pain that I've caused her, the fact she's finally letting me see it, gives me hope.

I pull her close and wipe her tears with my thumb; there are so many there's no way to stop them. I wish I had more light, I want to see her eyes. I need to see her eyes.

"I didn't leave, Nicole. You didn't know I was there, but every night I laid with you. I held you and Dom in my arms. *I didn't leave Mama*, I couldn't leave you if I tried, woman. You *own* me."

"I'm scared, Dragon. I won't survive if you pull shit like this again."

My stomach turns at the amount of pain coming from my woman. If I could go back I would…Is there a way to fix this?

"So that's it, Nicole? You want to end it, end us? You don't even want to *try*?"

Just the words hurt me. What do I do if she says she

227

doesn't? Can I let her walk away? *Fuck*. Can I give her up?

"Dragon," she whispers so lightly, it's almost silent. Her voice shaky and her body is straining to just breathe. Guilt and sadness come down on me. *I broke her.*

"Get in the car. I'll take you home…I'll take you back to your car."

She doesn't respond, her head goes down and just the picture of her standing like this, in the dark, is painful. When she makes no move to get back in the car I pick her up. She lies against me boneless.

"I'm sorry Mama, I'm so fucking sorry," I whisper under my breath. I haven't cried since Nicole was shot. Tears make you weak. Right now, I could easily give in and join my woman. *Except, she's not my woman anymore.*

We drive in silence back to her car. I call Bull and tell him not to worry about getting Nicole's car. The air is thick with emotion.

"If it's alright, I'd like to spend some time with Dom when he comes home. You can let me know when a good time is."

"Dragon, you can see Dom anytime."

"Whatever…Nicole."

I pull back into the parking structure and follow the arrows like a robot, parking beside her car with a sense of dread.

"So, this is it?" She asks.

She sounds surprised and for the life of me I can't figure out why. It pisses me off. I've done everything and jumped through hoops for this woman. So, I fucked up. I know that. It hurt her, but Jesus Christ, what more can I do here?

I lay my head on the steering wheel and try to get control of my emotions. *It doesn't work.*

"What the fuck do you want from me, Nicole? Seriously? I've apologized, I've begged, fuck, I've given you everything you want. I've fought to keep us together. You're the one that has been telling me for months that you needed time away, you're the one who moved out, and you're the one shutting me out. What the fuck do you expect from me here? Don't you think you already have my dick chopped off enough, panting after your ass? What the fuck more could I possibly give you?"

She just stares at me, her eyes large in disbelief.

"Fuck this shit. If this is what love does to you, it's no fucking wonder I never bothered."

"You're being an asshole," she says, but I'm so sick and tired of hearing the pain in her voice, like she is blameless in this shit. So, I let it all hang out.

"Yeah that's me, Mama. A fucking asshole right? I mean it's not like my woman didn't *hide* a whole fucking life and *lie* to me from day one. It's not like, instead of telling me when shit was about to hit the fan, she kept her damn secret and threatened to *leave* me. It sure as hell has nothing to do with the fact that my woman had me and my men jump through hoops and put on fucking clothes that we would *never* wear, for the privilege of putting my ring on her hand, just to fucking leave me standing on the damn sidewalk! I mean what the hell, right? You're the only one that's been hurt and wronged in this situation. Right, Nicole? So, I had a friend blown up in front of me, what's the big deal? So I had to watch him burn and make decisions quickly—again big-fucking-deal. You want to bitch because I didn't consult you? Maybe if you hadn't left me there standing on the fucking sidewalk and been with me you would have known. You ever think of that, Nicole? Still, like the motherfucking fool I am, I can't breathe without you so I repeatedly slam my head against a damned brick wall trying to get you to let me back in. Now, you sit there and ask me if this is it and call me an asshole. Yeah, Mama, this is it. I am done. There's only so much a man is willing to crawl, even for your golden pussy."

She gasps and then her hand comes out to slap me. I grab her wrist, by reflex.

"I'm sorry I even tried to get through to you!" She growls, yanking her hand away and turning to open the door.

She's not going to get the final word. *Oh hell no.* I get out and face her.

"You didn't try shit! You already had your mind made up we were done. You're just enjoying getting your revenge!"

"My revenge? Are you crazy? What the hell are you talking about?"

"You got your panties in a twist. So you want to see me hurt, like I hurt you. I get it, Nicole. I do. Go ahead and rip my fucking heart out, leave me and take my son. Throw me away yet again, like yesterday's garbage. I'm done begging you to stay!"

"Oh will you quit saying that to me. You are not garbage!"

"Then what am I, Mama? What the fuck am I?"

"I…" she stops, her eyes wide and her forehead

creased in confusion.

"You're…home," she says and the words are such a drastic change from the argument we are having that I have to stop and replay her words in my head.

"Mama?" I ask confused on if we're still fighting or what the hell just happened. I think the fucking woman just gave me whiplash.

"You're home, Dragon," she says again, her eyes wide. She's breathing hard, her hair is fanned around her face and down her shoulders.

I don't think, I'm pretty sure that's impossible right now, anyway. I grab her by the back of the neck and slam my mouth against hers. Her hands come up pulling on my cut, at the same time I take her mouth. She pushes my cut off my arms and I maneuver so it falls to the fucking ground. I don't give a damn. My hands reach the silk blouse she's wearing and I rip it apart. Buttons pop and fly out of the way at the same time her hands lift my shirt up. I yank it over my head. Our lips break apart, only because I have no choice, as the shirt joins my cut on the concrete.

"Fuck, Mama…." I hiss as her nails bite into my sides. I feel the soft skin of her stomach slide against mine.

"Dragon, I need you." She moans before our lips come back together. My hand goes to the button of her jeans, undoing it and sliding the zipper down.

"I got you Mama, I got you." I mumble, my lips kissing down her neck, my fingers slide into her underwear and immediately delve into her depths.

She's so fucking wet, my dick is pounding against my jeans—demanding to come out and play. I slip my fingers against her soaked clit torturing it and she bites into my shoulder. *Motherfucker*, I need inside of her now. I pull back just enough so I can slide her clothes down over her hips. My hand goes to my belt, fumbling around like a fucking teenager, when Nicole pushes against my chest.

"No…" she growls.

I jerk back. My dick is free, I'm about to slide home and *now* when she wants to stop?

"Damn it, Mama…"

"We can't, not here, Dragon. Anyone can see."

It hits me we're in the middle of the hospital parking structure. If I listen, I can hear cars and voices. I try to breathe, because I can barely think. Blood is pounding in my system and I can hear it echoing in my ears. I'm at the point I don't care who is around, I'll take her on the fucking hood.

Finally, I spot the cement pillar behind us. I pick her up and carry her to it. I put her back against the stone, as her feet slide to the ground. My eyes hold hers.

"Take your clothes off."

I expect her to argue. I expect her to shoot me down. She doesn't. She kicks off her shoes and steps out of her clothes. She's buck naked from the waist down. Her shirt is open and torn all to hell, her breasts are heaving in a blue lace maternity bra and her skin is marked up from my rough kisses. *She's fucking phenomenal.* I'd crawl on hot coals to get to this woman, I know instinctively, I always will. Everything about her is perfect, and I get lost just staring at her.

"Are you going to fuck me or wait for everyone and their grandmothers to join us?" She asks.

I guess I might have been staring a little too long, but

fuck me it's been so long…

"Haven't you heard that the best things come to those who wait, Mama?" I ask, blanketing my body against hers, running my tongue along the outer shell of her ear, whispering my words, tasting the salty-sweet flavor of her skin.

"I'd be satisfied just to cum, Dragon. It's been too damn long," she says back, her voice thick with need.

I'd laugh but her hand wraps around my dick and positions it at her entrance, while her other hand tugs on my jeans and her hand flexes against my ass.

"Why do you get to keep your jeans on?"

"Why are you asking….questions? Jesus, Mama." I hiss out the last as I slide into her.

It has been too long—way too long. Her silky walls instantly stretch and welcome me, enclosing around my cock tightly. She whimpers and her teeth latch onto my neck.

"Too soon, Mama, we can stop?" I ask because it would kill me, but I'll pull out before I hurt her.

"If you do I'll kill you," she whispers into my ear.

Both her hands slide under my opened pants, and grab my ass, pulling me deeper.

"It's never close enough, Dragon. No matter how deep you get inside, it's never close enough."

She's right. She's fucking-absolutely right. It's always been that way. I wrap my hand around her knee and pull her leg up to my thigh, sinking in just a little more.

"Ohh….fuck, yeah. That feels so good," she moans.

I smile and take control. My woman has become more vocal since we've been apart. That's good to know. I pull back until my cock is almost completely unsheathed and then angle so I go back in differently, scraping her walls. I kiss her, thrusting my tongue in and claiming her mouth. Her tongue dances with mine, wild and fierce and hungry—just like her slick, tight pussy. I keep our mouths fused, as I pick up my pace. It's been so long and we're both so far gone, I know it won't take long. Still, I take my free hand and slide her bra down just enough I can tease her nipple. I pinch it hard, giving her a bite of pain, knowing they have to be tender. A touch of her milk glides against my fingers and right or wrong I fucking love it. I squeeze harder, releasing just a little more and use the wetness to slide over and over her nipple, all the while pounding into her. My balls are actually sore from the climax just waiting to explode, but somehow my woman is managing to hold on. I feel her walls flutter against me. She's ready, but she's holding back. I can't have that. My lips slide along the line of her jaw, up into the shell of her ear.

"Your pussy is so good, Mama. When we finish here I'm going to take you home and spread you out on the table in my office."

"You are…" she gasps as I pinch her nipple again.

"I've thought about it for months. I'm going to get out our toys and slide a nice, thick vibrator into that ass of yours, turn it up on high, and fuck you with it."

"Oh shit…Dragon… I'm….."

Her body jerks in reaction to my words, clamping so tight on my cock that my eyes nearly roll back in my head.

"All the time I'm doing that Nicole, I'm going to be eating your pussy over and over. I won't stop until you scream my name so loud you lose your voice."

With that last promise, Nicole detonates. One thrust... two...and then I join her.

Chapter 36

NICOLE

"I CAN'T BELIEVE we just did that in the middle of a hospital parking garage." I say, shaking my head—more at myself than him. Dragon doesn't care. He'd fuck me wherever and whenever, he's always been like that. Case in point, the way he smirks and smiles at my words like the fucking cat that ate the fucking canary. I shake my head even as my womb clinches, watching him slide his cock back into his pants and zipping up. I want him again.

"You keep looking at me like that, Mama and we're going to go for round two."

Shit.

"I think we've given people enough of a thrill," I return, thankful that no one seems to be around.

I get busy pulling my own clothes on and righting them. My shirt is a total disaster. I tie the ends and do my best to cover my boobs. Then I brush my fingers through my hair, knowing that's probably hopeless, too. I look up and see Dragon still has that same look on his face, but thankfully (or regretfully) he has his pants done up now.

Regretfully, girl. Definitely, regretfully. Bad Nicole chimes in. She seems to only speak these days when Dragon is around to prod her. Weird, I've missed her voice, too.

"What?" I ask when he doesn't move or speak, choosing instead to stare and make my knees weak.

"I'm pretty sure you scared anyone away when you screamed out my name, Mama. So, no worries."

I do my best to hide the smile I feel. I *mostly* succeed.

"You do realize we just had sex without protection?"

"Not wearing a glove with you, Mama, I love the feel of your pussy too fucking much."

"Hate to break it to you bad boy, but no more sex until you start wearing gloves. I'm going on birth control, but your soldiers are so damned stubborn we're being extra safe."

"Whatever you say, Mama." He says in such a way, I have no doubt his mind is made up and it's *not* because he's decided to go buy condoms.

"Fine. Then you can pull out," I grumble, bending down to pull the strap of my sandal over my heel. When I stand back up Dragon is right in front of me.

"Two things," he says, his voice is gravely in a tone he gets when we have sex. It sends chills through me and makes my nipples hard. How does that happen? As hard as I came, it should be impossible at least for a few minutes, right?

"Enlighten me," I say, trying to sound unaffected by him. I don't think I succeed. *I don't think any woman could.*

"One, I'm ecstatic, freaking over the moon that you plan on having sex with me again and I don't have to fight shit to get us there."

"Dragon…." He stops my reply with a finger on my lips. It should annoy me but instead, my inner hussy opens my mouth and sucks his finger inside.

His eyes go dark and swirly. So, good girl that I am? I suck harder and wrap my tongue around it. *Yum.*

"Jesus," Dragon mutters and I can't help but smile as I release his finger with a pop. He shakes his head.

"And two, mark this down, Nicole… I am not now, nor ever will be pulling out and giving up your warm, wet pussy, to leave my soldiers cold. Not going to happen. Unless it's to cum on your face and tits, so I can slide my cock in between them and go for round two…I might could for that," Dragon says, staring at my breasts like a drowning man looking at a life preserver that is just out of reach.

I close my eyes and picture what he is saying and swear that one touch could rocket me out of the stratosphere. This man is definitely my kryptonite.

I open my eyes to find him laughing. He picks me up and pushes me against my car. My legs go around him and my fingers plow into the hair on each side of his face. His eyes are lit up. Happy. Dragon is happy. It speaks to me. It makes me feel…*complete.*

"I've missed you, Mama. I've missed you so fucking much," he says, bending down to press our lips together. I open for him without thinking and the kiss is heated, but also sweet and slow. It's about the two of us being together again. It's the sweetest kiss I've ever had.

"We still need to figure some things out," I caution, because I may have decided to take a leap here, but both of us need to learn to open up to the other more.

With one last soft touch of our lips, he lets me slide back down his body. His hand brushes the side of my face, tucking some of my hair behind my ear.

"We will, Mama. Long as we do it together, I'm good."

"Forever," I promise.

His smile freezes and then kicks up another notch.

"Fuckin' A."

I laugh, shaking my head at him.

"You going to take me home and make good on your promise or what, Dragon?"

"Thinking I should definitely take you home."

He takes my hand into his and leads me over to the passenger side of his Tahoe.

"You know, you hardly ever ride your bike, lately. It's like I'm in love with just a regular guy with a nine to five job."

"Bite your damn tongue. It's because my woman hasn't been in any shape to ride with me."

"I think I just proved I can handle riding on your bike."

"Then tomorrow, unless we're needed for Dom, we will go for a ride. Just the two of us."

"To the Falls?" I ask excitedly, because it's been so long since we've done that.

"Anything you want, Mama," he says kissing my forehead. He opens the door and I slide in, feeling more my old self than I have since the day Michael Kavanagh's goon stood at mine and Dani's table.

"We do have one major problem, Dragon."

"Just one? Hell, we're practically home free now," he says mockingly.

"Sarcasm does nothing for you, sweetheart."

He shakes his head at me, putting the vehicle in reverse. We drive for a little bit before he finally asks me the question I've been waiting for.

"I give, what's our *major* problem, Mama?"

"We can't raise Dom at the club, sweetheart. I know it is home to you, but a baby needs a house to grow up in and I don't want my seven year old wandering out of his room to get a snack and see Twinkies getting it on with some of the men. That is just *not* going to happen."

Dragon goes silent and I worry a little, but I know I'm right. The club was fine when it was just him and me, but Dom deserves a home. A place to grow and be happy and loved in. All the things Dragon and I never had growing up.

"What if we build a house next to the compound, out back, away from the main grounds? We could put up a big privacy fence, so Dom would be protected from any of the craziness. Plus, it'd be close enough to be protected by the club and the defenses already in place."

I think about it. I like it. Plus, it'd be close enough that Dani could watch Dom when... shit... Dani.

"Okay, Mama, if you don't like that we'll start looking at houses close by."

"No, no sweetheart, I like the idea—honest. I was just thinking about Dani. I need to talk with her. I've not been nice to her lately."

"She understands. She loves you, Mama."

"I know…it's just…we have things to work through. I completely blamed her, and I shouldn't have. I made my own decisions."

"It will be okay, Mama," he says picking up our joined hands and kissing it.

"I know," I whisper and for the first time in a long time, I believe that.

"Dial Bull and put it on speaker, Mama," he says motioning to his phone.

I don't question, I just do it. Honestly, I like holding his hand. I need to be connected to him right now. There's a part of me that never wants to let him go again. I may have taken a leap, but that fear is still there.

I put the phone on my lap and dial the number. It's not exactly easy to dial with just one hand.

"Yo," Bull's voice comes over the phone.

"Hey man, have the boys pick up Nic's car after all."

"Damn man, you're starting to get annoying."

"Fuck you," Dragon says with a laugh.

"No thanks." Bull retorts.

"Asshole. Did you tell the boys about Church?"

"Yeah man, they want to do it tomorrow. Shit has been up in the air too long."

"Too fucking bad, I'm taking my woman to visit our son and then we're going out for the rest of the day. Tell them to shut that shit down. They can bitch Friday. I'm spending time with my woman."

"You got it."

The phone clicks off and I sit there looking out the window. I can't explain it. Maybe my hormones are still wonky, but the fact that he put me before a needed meeting with his men brings a few waterworks out.

"Mama?" He asks when I haven't spoken for a few minutes.

"Just thinking," I answer managing to keep the emotion from my words. "How come you need a meeting so urgently?"

Dragon sighs.

My heart drops, expecting to hear him tell me how it's club business, blah, blah, and freaking blah.

"Crusher. He went off on his own way too much. Put the club in jeopardy, left messes we still need to clean up. He fucked up and he called me out. If I don't address it Mama, I'll be viewed as weak."

I don't pretend to understand the way the club works—or hell, even men. I just nod. He's let me in. Something between us has completely shifted. It feels good. So, I lean over and kiss his cheek, while he's watching the road.

He spares a glance at me and there's a question in his eyes.

"Hurry home, sweetheart. I really want to see the church table."

His barking laughter somehow finishes warming me all the way to my soul. *I'm home.*

Chapter 37

DRAGON

I CAN REMEMBER a time when I did not dread church. When coming into my office and sitting around this damn table was relaxing, or at the very least, it felt like I was where I belonged. How long has it been since I had that emotion with church? Since before Irish and his crap-storm? Probably. It sure as hell isn't today. No, it's *definitely not* today.

My hand moves over the table in front of me. I'd rather remember the way Nicole looked on this fucking table last night when I tongued that sweet pussy and made her scream, or even the day before. It was so good, I needed it again last night. Fuck, who am I kidding? I'm going to want it again tonight. Except maybe this time, I'll use the vibrator in her pussy while I fuck her ass. Fuck, my dick is throbbing and this meeting hasn't even started.

I look over at Crusher. I've had him locked in the cooler for the last few days. It is, in fact, a cooler—a walk-in freezer at the back of the club that went bad. We never fixed it because it just wasn't needed. The club has a couple of stand-up freezers they actually use. So when the walk-in went down it seemed to make a good cage. We modified it so air flow and temperature were regulated and turned into a holding cell. I sure as fuck never thought I'd have to throw my brother in it, especially my VP. That fucking shit sits raw in my gut and I know the men around me are unhappy. Which just means this meeting is going to be a fucking picnic of butterflies and lemon drops. That helps me get my libido under control, and I prepare to do what I have to do.

I drop the gavel. The men instantly stop their idle chatter. There wasn't much anyway. The importance of this meeting is too big.

"Meeting of the Savage MC, Kentucky Brothers called. On the table, the removal of club Vice President from rank. A vote was called. Let's hear from the brother first.

All eyes turn to Crusher. His eyes look at me and, fuck, I can barely see my brother in them. He looks wild…haunted. When he doesn't make a move to say anything, I prod him.

"Do you have nothing to say for yourself?"

"Bastard had my old lady, I handled shit that needed to be done. I got Dani back and I'd do it a fucking times over. If that gets me booted from the club then what-the-fuck-ever."

He says and he might look like shit, but his voice is full of cocky anger.

"You defied direct orders, and put the club in jeopardy. You put a woman before your brothers, and you had the fucking balls to call me out in front of others. I should strip you of club colors right here and close the fucking vote. *The end.*"

"She is not a woman, she is *my old lady.*"

"She hasn't agreed to that shit, so that makes her a *woman*."

"Bullshit. I claim her. My woman needed me. I did nothing more or nothing less than you would have done," he answers and shit, he's mostly right. Except I did handle it differently. I might not have though if Nicole and Dani had been taken in the same manner. I'm not fucking sure. Still, I can't really back down.

"He's right," Dani's weak voice comes from the door. Fucker, I want to yell at her for coming in during church. I want to cut off the prospect's balls for letting her, since he's in charge of watching the cameras at the front door and *locking* the son of a bitch when a meeting is taking place. I don't, because this is the first real sign of life Dani has shown. Oh, she's approached me alone since her attack, but to see her venture out into a room full of men? That takes balls of steel considering what she's been through. I look behind her and see Nicole is holding her hand and standing behind her. Bloody hell. *Vise meet my motherfucking balls.*

"What's that, Hell Cat?" Crusher asks. He gets up and goes to her. I just let it happen. Nicole has those damn girly tears in her eyes and there's only so much a man can do here.

I watch as Dani falters back a step, but she manages to stand still and look Crush in the eye.

"I admit that I am yours. I was yours then. I...I..."

"Say it, Hell Cat. Say it," Crusher says and the emotion in his voice is so thick, a man would have to be struck stupid to not to feel it.

"I'm yours now," she whispers, her voice so quiet you

can barely hear it.

Crush kisses her forehead gently.

"That's my angel," he whispers.

Dani has tears falling down her face, Nicole does too. Motherfucker, my club is turning soft. I shake my head in disgust, even though I'm happy with what has just happened.

"Go on back to your room angel, I'll check on you when we're done."

"But…," she argues looking at Crush and then around him at me. I can't give anything away, so I do my best to remain expressionless.

Crush touches her under the chin and brings her eyes back to his.

"I'm proud of you angel, don't worry. I'll do what I need to do and then I'll come to you."

She swallows slowly and nods before walking out of the room, with her head down.

"Hell Cat?"

She stops, but doesn't turn around.

"My woman doesn't look down. Remember?"

Dani's back stiffens and her head raises, "I won't forget."

"That's my girl."

"Just get your shit done, Zander, and quit busting my ass," she says.

It has none of the old fire that Dani used to have, but she gives a damned good attempt. I can't help but smile either. Nicole winks at me and I shake my head at her. The girls leave and the door closes. Crusher goes back to his seat, but motherfucker, the son of a bitch is crying. There are tears around his eyes and it seems so out of place on him. How long have I known Crusher? Longer than any of them, and I can't name one time when he's cried. He always appeared the laid back one, but Crusher is ice cold when it comes down to it. He always has been. *Fuck.* He's totally gone for Dani. From what I've just seen though, maybe that's what they both need. I clear my throat.

"Vote. Starting with Bull. Do we take Crush's patch? Aye or Nay, motherfuckers."

Crush sits staring every one of us straight in the eye.

"Nay," Bull says.

"Nay," Freak, Hawk and Dance join in.

"Nay," Nailer and Six join, having been patched in right after Frog's funeral. I breathe again. I didn't want rid of Crush, but a man has to do what is called upon him.

"Demotion of position. Aye or Nay?"

Bull stares at Crusher and the two exchange a wordless conversation of sorts before Bull sighs his answer, "Aye."

Hawk nods, "Aye."

Freak shakes his head, "Fuck, no."

Crush shoots him a half smile, but shakes his head.

Dance looks up at Crush and out of them all, his voice surprises me. "Nay. I'd have done the motherfucking same, man."

"Two for and two against. That leaves it in your hands Nail and Six."

"Fuck, sorry man. Aye," Nailer says. Crusher nods in response.

Six looks around shaking his head, "Son of a bitch, sorry man. Aye."

Demotion. I don't disagree with the vote. At the same

time, as much as I probably would have voted the same way, I'm not sure how I want to handle it. President has the final say, but I can't say I totally disagree, so I don't feel the need to override their decision.

Diesel, Skull and Torch would all sniff blood if they thought the club was weak. I can't let that shit stand. At the same time, if I was Crusher? Would I have handled things differently? I think on it.

I would have. Nicole is my woman and I'd move heaven and hell to get her back safe that is no doubt. Still, I would have made sure the club knew every move I made. I would never charge in without back up. I wouldn't kill without properly cleaning up my shit. Even if he had just burned the old barn down to get rid of the body, it would have been better.

"You charged into a hostile environment without calling on brothers for backup. You left a body for others to find without taking precautions to cover our asses. You called me out. You disrespected me in front of other clubs. You defied direct orders. I can't let it slide. *I won't*. Demotion granted."

Crusher nods with a grim smile. He expected it.

"Dance, you'll move up to VP. All those in favor say Aye."

A chorus of Aye's go through the room, including Crush's.

"Meeting adjourned," I growl, slamming the gavel against the table.

The men start filing out, all slapping Crusher on the back. Finally, when everyone has left Crusher remains sitting.

"Crush, man…"

"I get it brother, I'm not here to plead my case. I fucked up. I get it."

I nod, because fuck, what can I say?

"I need something from you and I realize I'm at the top of your shit list, but still I need this."

"Name it, brother."

"I need to leave."

"Damn it, Crush…"

"Not permanently. I'm going to take Dani away for a month. She needs to recover and she can't do that here. I don't want to leave the brotherhood man. I just need time to help my woman mend."

"She's it for you?"

"She's the motherfucking world."

I slap him on the back. "You got it then, man. Take her out to the club's house in Tennessee, on Douglas Lake. I'll clear it with Diesel."

"Thanks, Drag" he says getting up. "Man? For what it's worth? I'm sorry."

"I get it man. I got a woman, too."

He nods and walks to the door, he stops with the door halfway open. "Hey, Dragon? Kavanagh has a father. There could be blowback. My woman can't handle any more of that shit."

"Already being monitored."

"You'll let me know?" He asks.

"You'll be the first."

"Thanks, brother." He says and closes the door.

It opens a few minutes later and Nicole walks in and locks the door. She's wearing a baby blue sundress that matches her eyes. Her hair shines in the light. *Beautiful.*

"What are you doing here, Mama? Didn't you break rules enough coming in during the meeting?"

She walks over to me, her face soft.

"I thought you would be tense after your meeting. I wanted to offer to help." She says quietly, going to stand behind me massaging my shoulders.

"How you figure that?" I ask, closing my eyes.

She leans down so her lips are against my ear and whispers, "I thought this time I'd let you fuck me on the table."

My dick is definitely standing at attention now.

"Get on the table, Mama."

"You'll have to pull out though," she says, sitting up on the table. She lifts the dress over her head and I'm not a bit surprised to see she's butt-ass naked underneath.

"Told you how I feel about that, Mama," I argue already standing and taking my clothes off.

"I know. That's why you have to pull out, because ever since you mentioned it, I've thought of nothing else."

My dick stands up and cheers in reaction. *Fuck.*

Chapter 38

DRAGON

One week later

IT'S BEEN A long ass day. I'm bone tired. We brought Dom home today and had a welcome home party at the club. It was good, but instead of getting to be with my woman and son I'm trapped talking with Diesel. He's heading back to Tennessee tomorrow and Dani and Crusher will be going with him. I don't want my brother to go. We have shit to settle, but I think he needs the time away and I know Dani could use it. I'm hoping it helps them. I was against them two getting together, but maybe they'll settle each other down.

I open the door to our bedroom and immediately close and lock it. I lean against the door for a minute and drink in the peace that instantly surrounds me. When Nicole was staying at Dance's, the place was…empty. Just having Nicole here, her presence makes the entire place different.

I turn and see Nicole breastfeeding our child. It takes my air away. This is *mine*. What the fuck did I do? What did the man upstairs find in me that he thinks I deserve this? Hell, I'm jaded as the day is long. I've seen shit that would make lesser men checkout of life without a backward glance. Worse, I have done shit in life. I have so much motherfucking blood on my hands that I will never be clean. Still, with all of that, I have something in my grasp that is pure and beautiful. How the fuck did that happen? I can't begin to guess, but I'm sure not going to let it go. My world is wrapped up in this woman and our son.

"Dragon?" She questions and shit, I can't remember my own name, let alone anything else right now.

"I want to be here whenever you feed Dom, Mama."

"Not sure that's practical, sweetheart."

"Fuck, practical. I *need* to be here."

"Dragon? Are you okay?"

"Just when I think I've got to know how good life is with you Mama, something else happens."

"Drag…" She begins, while she moves our son from her breast and lays him against her chest and gently pats him. I don't let her finish.

"I'm not a praying man; I've seen too much and done too much. But every fucking day I want to get down on my knees and thank my maker for you. I was dead inside before you, Mama. *Dead.* You wouldn't stop until you uncovered the bullet holes and patched them, made them go away. Now? Fuck, woman. The sight of you feeding our child… To see evidence of the way you completely love me and our son not just once in a while, but with every breath you take… I don't have words. I don't have a way to tell you what you are to me, Nicole. I don't think the damn words have been invented. I love you is too easy, too small, to tell you what I feel. If I live to be a hundred and four there won't be a day that I don't need you to help me breathe."

My woman has tears in her eyes, when I finish. I don't know what I said. I do know it didn't say what I wanted it to. I'm too fucking rough around the edges to give her the flowery speech she deserves.

She walks over to the crib and lays Dom down. When she's done she comes to stand in front of me. Her hand slides against my face and her blue eyes shine with tears, but also with happiness.

"I love you, too. Forever."

"Forever," I promise, and it's more than a promise. *It's a motherfucking vow.*

She pulls my lips to hers and whispers, "Home." The words brush against my skin and I feel it all the way to my soul.

Epilogue

NICOLE

Two Months Later

MY MAN IS insane. He's been after me for months. He *wants* a wedding. After the disaster of our first go around, you would think that he would have had enough. I know I have. If I never see another wedding dress, worry about bridesmaids, hear another bridal march, or ever see my man in a suit again that would still be *too soon*. I decided we should just go on like we are. I don't need a piece of paper to tell me that Dragon and I belong to each other. *He*, however, refuses to go along with my plan. So after two months, he wore me down. I completely caved. Of course, I can admit that I did so after multiple orgasms. I lost count and maybe consciousness around number four. So, I agreed to anything he wanted. I only had one stipulation—*one major stipulation*. I told him it had to be the farthest thing from our first go around that he could find. I wanted nothing like that. I had regretted it way before the actual catastrophe at the church. Huge church weddings are *not* what Dragon and I are. I wanted the perfect ending to our fairy tale. What I didn't realize at the time, was Dragon and I aren't a fairy tale. We're real.

We're bigger. We're better. We're a freaking *never-ending* story, and it's epic.

So when Dragon said not to worry. I left it in his hands. The plane ride to Vegas wasn't a surprise. The fact that all the Savage Brothers came along, save for the prospects watching the place back home wasn't a surprise. The fact that Dani is here and smiling? It's good. It's not a surprise because she's been different since her and Crusher came home. I even see glimpses of that first beautiful girl who became my best friend years ago. The fact he has me pump extra milk so Dancer and Carrie can watch Dom tonight and part of the day tomorrow? Sweet, but not surprising. The limo ride to an all-night wedding chapel at eleven-thirty at night? Yeah, it didn't even surprise me. Dragon having a dress waiting for me in the dressing room? Again, not a surprise. I'll admit that when I saw I would be wearing a red leather dress, which was skin tight and ended barely below my thigh, a cut that said *Property of Dragon*, matching black stockings and a red garter clearly visible with my fuck-me boots? I might have been a teensy bit surprised. The fact that my bridesmaids were in matching ensembles, except they were all wearing black with red garters, might have shocked me. I can't lie. Then again, I'm figuring Dragon doesn't give a damn. I have to say all the girls are gorgeous and hot as hell, even Carrie—who looks like she might pop at any minute. Hell, I look hot. I admit it. Still, nothing has been a surprise (clothes not withstanding) and even though it *is* different, the very moment Dani, Carrie, Nikki, and Lips leave to join the men outside, I get scared. What if we're pushing it? What if fate doesn't want Dragon and me to get married? My heart starts beating like crazy, my palms go sweaty and I'm barely keeping it together. That's when I hear it.

It's a scream, melodic but a scream none the less and then the guitar rift kicks in and the music starts. I stand for a minute trying to place the song. When I do, I throw my head back in laughter. Just like that, the nerves are gone and I leave the room anxious to see my crazy ass husband-to-be.

I walk to a red silk covered aisle to the song *'Heaven's on Fire'*, by Kiss. I'm still laughing, but when I look down at the end of the small runway and see my man standing beside what I can only assume is a Gene Simmons look-alike—with makeup, I lose it. I feel a touch on my arm and look up to see a very handsome Bull standing there with one single black rose. The color doesn't shock me at all this time. How can it, when all of the Savage MC and their women are standing in front of me wearing leather and cuts. My man is standing tallest of them all, holding Dom in his hands. My baby is in pajamas that reads, I then a big red heart with mom under it. I take the flower and link my arm in with Bull's and walk towards my future.

When I make it to my man, he hands Dom over to Dancer. Dom protests just once before Dance produces his favorite squishy rattle. I give my rose to Dani and when I turn back around Dragon is staring down at me with this smile on his face and I get lost in the deep, chocolatey depths of his eyes.

"You're looking good, Mama."

"You are so crazy, Dragon."

"You asked for different, I aim to please."

"I love you," I answer. I'm so happy, I feel like I might

explode.

"Are you ready to do this?"

"Completely."

We turn together to face the...err...*Gene Simmons?*

"Dear freaks and psychos we are gathered here tonight to celebrate the union of Dragon and Nicole, so let's get this party started. Nicole, do you promise to always take care of Dragon's *Love Gun?* Do you promise to worship at the altar of *Detroit, Rock City, Forever?* He asks, using titles of Kiss songs, which at this point doesn't surprise me at all.

"Love Gun?" I question Dragon and he is smiling as big as I've ever seen.

"Hey, women like it when a man writes the vows, right?"

I shake my head, taking the ring Dani hands me and slipping it on Dragon's finger, "I promise to love you and stay by your side, forever."

Dragon kisses my forehead.

"Dragon?" Fake Gene questions and I expect more silly song title vows, instead, Dragon's gets serious and he caresses the side of my face.

"Nicole, I was lost until you came into my life with that rocking ass and those sexy bare feet. I fell fast and hard and I've never looked back. You keep me grounded, Mama. You give me a reason and a purpose to keep going. You are my life. You are the air I fucking breathe, woman. I promise I will love you in this world and into the next. I promise that I will protect, honor and spend my life doing my best to make you and Dom happy. *Forever Mama, for-fucking-ever,"* he says quietly, sliding a simple gold band on my finger that has a D and N engraved on it with a diamond in the middle of the interlocked letters.

I don't even try to stop the tears that come.

"I love you, Dragon. I love you so much."

"Does that mean I did okay?"

"Well, I did miss the hokey song titles and all," I joke through my tears.

"Hmmm… I promise I will *Lick It Up*, and *Uh! All Night*. That better, Mama?"

I can't answer but then everyone around is laughing, so it's not needed.

"Alright! If I can have your hands?" Fake Gene asks and Dragon and I turn around to face him.

Fake Gene takes our hands, places his over them.

"Then by the power invested in me by the State of Nevada, I pronounce you man and wife! Time to kiss the bride!" He yells and starts wiggling his tongue like crazy.

"Mama!" Dragon growls.

"He really is just like Gene. I didn't realize they made tongues that….What are you doing?" I gasp as Dragon picks me up and throws me over his shoulder. Everyone in the room is laughing.

"Taking you back to our room to show you the only fucking tongue you'll ever need."

My man, he always has the best ideas.

The End

At least for now!

Read on for a personal note from the author as well as a glimpse of Claiming Crusher coming August, 2015.

Dear Readers,

I hope you enjoyed this book as much as I did. As mentioned, I never meant for this book to develop in the way that it did. Sometimes, the characters have wills of their own, and I find I enjoy it much more when they do. Because of the way Nicole bloomed though, it changed previous plans for Claiming Crusher (and this is why I don't write by outline).

Claiming Crusher's timeline takes place at the same time as Loving Nicole, and though the book starts with the past, so you get to know the characters, the actual chapters will start two weeks before Nicole and Dani were warned that Michael was lurking. I try to make my books standalones and for the most part they still are, but Loving Nicole weaves the series and future spin-offs together. For instance, Diesel is screaming for his own story and I'm dying to write it. So, with the time line in mind, please read on for a glimpse of Claiming Crusher.

J

The End of *Her*

MELINDA

I DON'T KNOW what sets him off this time. I honestly don't. I'm always so careful—the past year has *taught* me to be careful. I don't argue, I don't question. I make sure everything he could possibly want or ask from me is within easy reach. The cook knows the menu a solid week in advance. All meals are approved by Michael. In fact, everything is approved by Michael right down to the color of my hair and the pale, pink lip gloss I wear. I do not make a move unless it is approved by him.

I've been doing this for so long now, it has become second nature. I am almost robotic with it all. So, I honestly have no idea why I'm being summoned into Michael's office. My hands are shaking and a cold, clammy sweat pops out over my body. My stomach flutters nervously and I'm glad I haven't eaten. I'm standing outside Michael's office in our home and I'm terrified to knock, because I *know* what will happen. If I don't knock? If I try to run away? Michael will make me *pay*. I know, because I've done it in the past. I've learned not to run now—it hurts less. I stiffen my backbone and knock gently. I send up a prayer that he will be asleep or gone. As usual, the prayer goes unanswered. God forgot me long ago. I'm not sure he ever remembered me.

"Come in, Melinda." Michael says through the closed door. His voice sounds bored, tired even. I know better. The monster inside of him is pacing quickly back and forth, waiting to pounce.

I walk in without a word. I still the shaking in my hands so I can gently shut the door. I walk to the chair in front of the desk, keeping my head down and avoiding eye contact. When I sit down and notice the green silk, slip dress I have on, I panic. Michael doesn't like green. He prefers me to wear light pastels. I have closets full of pink, lavender, and yellow. Those are acceptable colors. I have on the green dress because Michael was to be gone today. Is that what upset him? I'm so *stupid*! Why do I even keep this dress?

"It would appear we have a problem, Melinda," he begins calmly. It's as if he is talking about the weather. Then again, Michael is always calm. Even when he is doling out punishment, his voice never raises. It stays in a clipped, concise, and in a proper tone. That somehow makes him scarier, to me.

"I'm sorry," I say by reflex. I don't know what I've done, it *doesn't matter* what I've done.

"I'm afraid that's not good enough considering your crime."

My *crime*. He always uses that term, as if he is judge, jury and executioner in charge and I the repeat offender. I want to ask what I did. It's on the tip of my tongue to question. I don't, I bite my tongue and concentrate on the pain instead. When I make no move to question him further, Michael lets off a loud sigh. The sound is one of annoyance. Annoyance from Michael and directed at me, only means bad things. I can't stop the way my heart kicks into overdrive, or the apologies which immediately spring up and rest on my lips. I don't give them voice, I beat them back. You can't show the monster weakness, he smells it and devours you. I pull my eyes from my shoes, to look out the window. I search for the sun outside. I'm not free, but if I can concentrate on the warm glare of the sun it will help—another lesson I've learned over the last year. I try to focus my breathing and that's when I see *it*.

On his desk is a tube of carnal, red lipstick. I love it and I sneak and put it on when I am alone. I dream of a day when I can wear this color all the time. I'm not brave enough to buy it. No, I'm not sure I have any bravery left in me. It was a gift from Nicole. I try to keep nothing out in the open of Nicole or my time at Three Oaks. Nicole might have hated the place, but I loved every minute of it. If only because it allowed me to stay away from Michael. When his lawyers found a judge they could buy and had that portion of my father's will overturned, *hell* truly began for me. I had no choice but to marry Michael and move in with him. I tried running. I *tried* and *failed*. I have the scars to prove it.

So, I stored away the good memories I had. Most of which, admittedly, revolve around Nicole. I risk a lot just to remain in contact with Nic, but she is my lifeline. If I don't hear her voice at least once a week, I feel hopeless. I can't let hope fade. If I give in…I'll never survive. Then, Michael will truly win.

How did he find the lipstick? I'm always so careful. I rack my brain trying to remember where I would have left it. Then I see it. The small, wooden box I keep hidden in the air conditioning vent in my closet. Inside are my most prized possessions. I may have been the Marinetti Shipping heir, but I had nothing unless Michael provided it. No, my most prized possession would bring you nothing at an auction. They consist of four things. Four things that mean everything to me.

First was the lipstick Nicole gave me. Next was a note from my father. The very last note I ever got from him. I don't know *why* I keep it. I hate him for what he did to me. There's a picture of me and Nicole in one of those silly photo booths at a town fair. It was probably the best day I've ever had in my life. Finally, there is the one thing in this world that I need to survive. The one thing I touch every night. My mother's medallion. She gave it to me before she died. It's my last connection to my mother. I can't lose it. *I can't.*

My heart stops. The monster has them. I know he won't give them back. He will destroy them, just to prove a point. He will relish the fact that he is hurting me. A hundred words come to my lips, words I could use to beg him to give me my things back. I clinch my hands in tight fists, letting my nails bite into my skin. I can't beg. Begging him only incites him to go further, to be meaner. I remain quiet, waiting.

"Have you nothing to say, Melinda?"

"I am sorry, Michael."

"Is there some reason you have kept these things hidden from me, my darling wife?"

The fake sugary-sweetness he uses when calling me his wife causes the acid in my stomach to boil. How much hate can one person hold in their body? There are times, when I think I have nothing but hate.

How do I answer here? Do I tell him I didn't want him touching them? That if he did, he would somehow taint them? Do I lie and say they are unimportant? I'm honestly at a loss on how to answer.

In the end, I shrug and try playing down the whole thing.

"They are just memories of my childhood. Nothing that important Michael," I answer, trying to inject sincerity into my words.

Michael comes around in front of me leaning on his desk. His arms are crossed and he looks so relaxed. I know what's coming though. I know what always happens when I do something to displease the monster. The sick feeling inside of me floods through my bloodstream. Will he kill me this time? He's come close before. Will tonight be the final end of it all? I think I'd be okay if it was. I need it to end. I can't keep going like this. *I'm tired.*

Acknowledgments

By book three you would think I have this author thing figured out right? You forget I'm blonde. There are way too many people to thank, and I'm trying to get better and condensing so I don't bore everyone. So, let me begin by giving a blanket thank you to my Street Team and the woman who runs it Neringa. Those girls blow my mind daily with their laughter, their encouragement and their friendship. There's not a one of them I don't love and appreciate.

Kurt Gangluff I miss you daily. Thank you so much for the encouragement and friendship.

Thank you to Margreet Asselbergs with Rebel and Edit designs for designing and re-designing this cover. It's not easy to go against what is mainstream. It's much harder to go against the grain of what is expected in an MC book. I will not lie though, this is my favorite cover to date and I would have messed it up completely had Margreet not held steady and strong and taught me to go with my gut.

Thank you to Sabrina Paige. For your mentorship certainly, but more importantly for your friendship. My day is empty if I go without at least saying hi to you.

Thank you to Sam Crescent. I was panicking and you calmed me. I was thinking of not writing again and you calmed me. You my friend are just an amazing human being and a kick-ass author. To even be able to say I have spoken with you means the world, because your books kept me sane when Poppy was dying. I am still and will forever be star-struck. (The same could be said for your partner in crime Jenika Snow).

Thank you to Jen Wildner of Just One More Page for being so amazing in everything you do for authors, and for holding my hand, encouraging me and making me laugh. I love you to infinity and beyond.

Thank you to Fran Owens and CJ Fling for editing and being here every step of the way. I love you women.

Thank you to Mayra Stratham for just being a totally amazing human being and friend.

Thank you to Jess Peterson for your friendship, your encouragement and for running kick-ass parties. I can't wait to see how fantastic your new business will be. Though I miss your touch and help with my books, I have all the faith in the world in you and can't wait to see your business explode! Love you Big.

Thank you to Krissy Gentry, Tami Czenkus, Corry Parnese, LaVida Brisco and Echo Clayton for your laughter, your support and most of all for being my friend.

KA Matthews you were phenomenal in your help with this book. I wish you every success with your new venture!

Dessure Hutchins I love you from your Double D's to your tiny ass and your sexy toes. No words express how much you mean to me.

Nicole Panepinto Violino and Andrea Florkowski you two have so much to deal with and you do so with laughter, grace and a kick ass attitude. You inspire me.

Tammie Smith. I can't! There just aren't words to

thank you for what you have done and how tirelessly you work. You are my lifeline some days. I love you to the moon and back again and beyond because there are no limits. I love you Wonder Twin.

I said I was going to condense—I failed. There are so many more authors and bloggers and friends, if you didn't get mentioned just know I was afraid to start in case I forgot someone! For everything you've done to help me, you have my gratitude and devotion. I love you all.

Jordan.

Loving Nicole Playlist

open.spotify.com/user/12149197675/playlist/1p4Kgn2s29r8ywpOTHWpvr

Saving Dancer Playlist

open.spotify.com/user/12149197675/playlist/1uMJhzmhkKYLeWWW7aBZZX

Breaking Dragon Playlist

open.spotify.com/user/12149197675/playlist/1JWfJFpsf4odID9kgVULlV

Author Links!

Spotify:

open.spotify.com/user/12149197675/playlist/1JWfJFpsf4odID9kgVULlV

Facebook: facebook.com/jordanmarieauthor

Pinterest: pinterest.com/jordanmarieauth

Twitter: twitter.com/Author_JordanM

Goodreads:
goodreads.com/author/show/9860469.Jordan_Marie

Amazon:
www.amazon.com/Jordan-Marie/e/B00RY72I2U

Webpage: jordanmarieauthor.weebly.com

Sign up for my newsletter and never miss news about upcoming sales, new releases, and exclusive sneak peeks and giveaways!
Newsletter: eepurl.com/barBKv

Previous Titles:

Breaking Dragon Savage Brothers MC Volume 1
Saving Dancer Savage Brothers MC Volume 2

Made in the USA
Middletown, DE
15 February 2020

84845641R00155